安徽省高校人文社会科学研究重点项目 "19 世纪末至 20 世纪 20 年代唐诗英译研究"（项目编号：SK2018A0529），安徽省高校优秀青年人才支持计划项目 "英语世界的唐诗译介研究"（项目编号：gxyq2018088）

Translation of Tang Poetry's Images
in the Comparison of Chinese and Western Culture

中西文化对比下的唐诗意象英译

周蓉蓉　著

吉林大学出版社

·长春·

图书在版编目（CIP）数据

中西文化对比下的唐诗意象英译 = Translation of Tang Poetry's Images in the Comparison of Chinese and Western Culture / 周蓉蓉著.— 长春 ： 吉林大学出版社，2020.4

ISBN 978-7-5692-6291-9

Ⅰ．①中… Ⅱ．①周… Ⅲ．①唐诗－英语－翻译－研究 Ⅳ．① I207.22 ② H315.9

中国版本图书馆 CIP 数据核字（2020）第 057133 号

书　　名：中西文化对比下的唐诗意象英译

Translation of Tang Poetry's Images in the Comparison of Chinese and Western Culture

作　　者：周蓉蓉　著
策划编辑：邵宇彤
责任编辑：代景丽
责任校对：柳　燕
装帧设计：优盛文化
出版发行：吉林大学出版社
社　　址：长春市人民大街4059号
邮政编码：130021
发行电话：0431-89580028/29/21
网　　址：http://www.jlup.com.cn
电子邮箱：jdcbs@jlu.edu.cn
印　　刷：三河市华晨印务有限公司
成品尺寸：170mm×240mm　　16开
印　　张：9.25
字　　数：130千字
版　　次：2020年4月第1版
印　　次：2020年4月第1次
书　　号：ISBN 978-7-5692-6291-9
定　　价：39.00元

Foreword

As the gem of Chinese literature, classical poetry is famous for its terseness and implicitness due to the use of delicate image. Within brief lines, a poem can express the poet's affectionate emotion or a profound philosophy. Scholars at home and abroad have made lots of researches on the theory and practice of poetry translation with fruitful achievements. However, foreign scholars tend to make mistakes in the translation of Chinese classical poetry due to their lack of Chinese culture while at home the translation of classical poetry has not been guided by any systematic theory though fruitful achievements have been made. Equivalence Theory is founded on the basis of mature linguistics and has sound system. Its key concepts of "the closest natural equivalence" and "equivalent effect" have reasonability, feasibility and popularity in regular translation, including that of Chinese classical poetry.

So far most translation theories or ideas try to give a macro analysis to poetry translation as a whole. However, poetry is an organic mixture of national language and culture, consisting of form, content and style and covering aesthetics, history, philosophy and religion, etc. Western

Sinologist Arthur Waley stated that "image is the soul of poetry", and Hu Yinglin during Ming dynasty once said that "the essence of ancient poetry lies in image". Image in poetry is rich of cultural implications so that it can help to understand the poem on one hand but may enhance the difficulty of its translation on the other hand. In addition, Chinese classical poetry has a long history with a large quantity and Tang Dynasty witnesses its zenith. This is why cultural image in classical poetry during Tang period is chosen to be the research object from the perspective of Equivalence Theory.

This book has six chapters altogether. Chapter 1 is an introduction, mainly including literature review research significance of this topic. Chapter 2 is a clarification of Equivalence Theory of translation. Chapter 3 is an analysis of cultural image and its translation from the perspective of Equivalence Theory. Cultural image is proved to be the soul of classical poetry. Exemplified by the translation of Tang poetry, semantic equivalence and aesthetic equivalence of cultural image are claimed to be the basic requirement and ideal standard of cultural image translation respectively. Chapter 4 is to explore the strategies of cultural image translation: preservation of the original image with cultural overlap, adaptation of the original image with cultural parallelism, amplification of the original image with cultural deficiency and omission of the original image with cultural insignificance. Chapter 5 is to focus on comparison among some influential translators' works on their methods of image translation. Chapter 6 is the conclusion part.

In the background of "Chinese culture's going outside", qualified individual translators at home and abroad are to actively participate in promoting the cultural complementary in the world besides the government's support and participation. Due to the fact that my knowledge is poor and limited, the research I have made is very superficial, I hope experts as well as colleagues' suggestions and criticism could enlighten me.

CONTENTS

Chapter 1 Introduction

According to *Encyclopedia Britannica*, poetry is a literary genre that evokes a concentrated imaginative awareness of experience or a specific emotional response through language chosen and arranged, for its meaning, sound and rhythm. Poetry represents writing in its most compendious and condensed form, together with a quality of musicality to create unparalleled artistic charm. Poetry is the expression of man's thoughts and feelings, and the picture of man's sense and imagination. Chinese classical poetry has a long history of several thousand years, and the ancient poems are mainly songs which depict the scene of laboring or express the patriotic emotion. It has undergone various changes and gradually formulated its unique characteristics in rhyme scheme, choice of words, grammatical structure and rhetorical artistry, etc. The translation of Chinese classical poetry, though incomparable to the translation of foreign poetry, has been blooming rapidly and steadily during nearly the last century. The whole English versions of both *The Book of Poetry* (《诗经》) and *The Elegies of Chu* (《楚辞》) have come out; and especially the Tang poetry has been translated into the most important foreign languages; and the translation of classical poetry during Song and Yuan dynasties has achieved a lot. The translation of Chinese classical poetry by scholars at home and abroad is quite fruitful in practice, but comparatively short of scientific and systematic theoretical guidance. Hence it deserves more exploration.

1.1 Important Translators of Chinese Classical Poetry and Their Representative Works or Theories

In the process of spreading Chinese culture to the West, Tang poetry became the forerunner of cultural transmission. According to data, the translation and introduction of Chinese poems in the United Kingdom can be traced back to the earliest poems containing English introduction and translation of Tang poems, including *Translations from the Original Chinese with Notes* (《中文英译》) by British sinologist Robert Morrison (1782–1834). However, this book is not a monograph on Tang poetry. Morrison translated Du Mu's poem *Ascending the Mountain on the Nine Days* (《九日齐山登高》) at the end of the first part of the book. The quality of such a translation is very limited and the translator may not have paid much attention to it at the time, but it is the first complete English-language Tang poetry with available literature up to date.[1]

The Scottish missionary Dr. James Legge (1815–1897) was also one of the well-known sinologists who tried to translate Tang poetry earlier. Legge was sent to China by the London Missionary Society. In the 25 years

---

[1] 江岚, 罗时进. 早期英国汉学家对唐诗英译的贡献 [J]. 上海大学学报 (社会科学版),2009,16 (2):33–42.

from 1861 to 1886, all the major Chinese classics such as *the Four Books and the Five* (《四书五经》) Classics were translated into a total of 28 volumes.[①] From 1861 to 1872, Legge compiled a five-volume selection of Chinese classical poems, *The Chinese Classics* (《中国经典》), which also includes Tang Dynasty poetry.[②] For a long time, his translation was the definitive standard translation in the West.

Herbert A. Giles (1845–1935), a professor of Chinese studies at the University of Cambridge who was a British consul in China and authored a Chinese-English Dictionary, was the first to systematically translate Tang poetry into the English grammar school. Giles' first English translation of Chinese poems, *Chinese Poetry in English Verse*, was published in London and Shanghai at the same time in 1898. This anthology includes 101 Tang poems, including poems of Li Bai, Du Fu, and others translated into rhymes.[③] The poems used in the anthology have some accomplishments, such as Chang Jian's *Dhyana's Hall* (《题破山寺后禅院》).[④]

The famous British sinologist, L. Cranmer Byng (1872–1945), enjoyed the reputation of "expert of Chinese ancient poetry" in Europe and America. *A Lute of Jade* (《玉琵琶》) and *A Festival of Lanterns* (《灯笼节》) are the representative translations of his Chinese poems. *A Lute of Jade* was first published in 1909, and has been reprinted for more than 30 times.

---

① 何寅,许光华.国外汉学史[M].上海:上海外语教育出版,2002: 208.

② 王辉.理雅各与《中国经典》[J].中国翻译,2003(2): 37–41.

③ 张晓.唐诗英译实践及理论研究回顾[J].安徽文学,2011(9): 195–196.

④ 朱炳荪.读 Giles 的唐诗英译有感[J].外国语,1980(2): 43–44.

After *A Festival of Lanterns* was published by John Murray in 1916, it was reprinted by many publishers. In addition, in 1904, Cranmer Byng published *the Book of Odes* (《诗经》) in London. Although the number of Tang poetry translated by Cranmer Byng is not large, it has a great influence and promoted the spread of Du Fu's poetry in English translation at that time.[①]

When it comes to literary work of Tang poetry's English translation, the author should be British W. J. B. Fletcher (1871-1933). He came to China in the early twentieth century and worked as an interpreter at the British consulate. From the 34th year of the Qing Emperor Guangxu (1908), he served as British deputy consul and consul in Fuzhou, Qiongzhou, Haikou and other places. After retiring, he was a professor of English at Guangzhou Sun Yat-Sen University. Fletcher studied the English translation of Tang poetry. His translations include *Gems of Chinese Verse* (《英译唐诗选》) (also called as *The Essence of Chinese Poetry* 《中国诗歌精华》)with 181 Tang poems, published in 1919. *More Gems of Chinese Verse* (《英译唐诗选续集》) was published in 1925 with 105 translated Tang poems.[②] The famous British sinologist and literary translator Arthur Waley (1888-1966) was the most outstanding Orientalist in the 1950s. He was also the most outstanding translator who translated Oriental languages into English. There are more than 200 translations, most of which are related to Chinese culture. Most

---

① 李特夫. 20 世纪英语世界主要汉诗选译本中的杜甫诗歌 [J]. 杜甫研究学刊, 2011(4): 79-86.
② 江岚, 罗时进. 唐诗英译发轫期主要文本辨析 [J]. 南京师大学报 (社会科学版), 2009(1): 119 -125.

of the Chinese literary works he translated were Tang poetry, including *Selected Translations of Ancient Chinese Poems*. In addition, there are *A Hundred and Seventy Chinese Poems* (《中国古诗 170 首》) (including 59 poems by Bai Juyi) published in London in 1918 and *More Translations from the Chinese Poems* (《中国古诗选译续集》) in 1919. [①]In the translation, Waley used the method of literal translation to keep its original meaning of the poems. In order to retain the sense of rhythm in Chinese poetry, he tried to make use of stress in the English words corresponding to Chinese words, that is, according to remain the meaning and importance of the verse , which is not equivalent to the syllables inherent in the English words, forming the so-called "sprung rhythm" . He also tried to retain the images in the poems, so that many fresh Chinese poetic images entered the mind of the Westerners for the first time.[②]

Herbert A. Giles published his famous *A History of Chinese Literature* (《中国文学史》) in 1901, which included Tang poems, such as *The Everlasting Regret* (《长恨歌》) translated by him. In 1922, it was republished in Shanghai that a revised and extended version of its Chinese translation of the ancient Chinese poems, *Gems of Chinese Literature* (《古文选珍》) of 1844, was republished in Shanghai, including Bai Juyi's *The Song of a Lute* (《琵琶行》); In 1935 Waley published the English translation of *Selected Chinese Verses* (《中国歌诗选》) by the Shanghai Commercial Press. This book is divided into two parts, the first part translated by Giles, and the second part translated by Waley.

---

① 梁家敏 . 阿瑟· 韦利为中国古典文学在西方打开一扇窗 [J]. 编辑学刊 , 2010(2): 66-68.
② 缪峥 . 阿瑟·韦利与中国古典诗歌翻译 [J]. 国际关系学院学报 , 2000(4): 50-56.

The translation of the famous American poet Ezra Pound (1885–1972) has greatly promoted the development of English translation of Tang poems in the Western world. He published a collection of poems in London in 1915 under the title of *Cathay* (《神州集》). This collection of poems was later included in *the Poetry of Great Poets* by T. S. Eliot (1888–1965) and widely circulated in the West.[1] Among them are 14 poems of the Tang Dynasty, including Wang Wei's *Seeing Yuan the Second off to the Northwest Frontier*, Lu Zhaolin's *Chang'an Ancient Ideas*.[2] *Cathay* is a beautiful way to reproduce the artistic conception of Chinese ancient poetry from the aspects of language and image. Pound also proposed translation standards such as "faithfulness" and "authenticity" . The details of image in poetry cannot be ignored.

Since 1920, the American poet Witter Bynner (1881–1968), a former teacher of the University of California and the chairman of the American Poetry Association, has collaborated with Kiang Kanghu (1883–1954), *The Jade Mountain* (《群玉山头》) , which is the first English translation of *Three Hundred Poems* of the Tang Dynasty compiled by Heng Tang Tuishi,[3] and its style is between rhyme and free verse. Since it was published in 1929, it has been republished many times, which has a great influence and has made Tang poetry widely disseminated and accepted in the English-speaking world. It has also made an excellent model for Chinese-foreign cooperation

---

① 方华文. 20 世纪中国翻译史 [M]. 西安：西北大学出版社，2005: 426.

② 周建新. 庞德的《神州集》与中国古典诗歌现代化 [J]. 华北电力大学学报（社会科学版），2010(3): 107–113.

③ 马祖毅. 中国翻译通史 [M]. 武汉：湖北教育出版社，2006: 126.

in translating poems. Rexroth praised the translation as one of the finest poems in America in the 20th century.[1]

Since the 1970s and 1980s, the United States has become the center of translation and study of Tang poetry in the Western world. Today, the most representative Tang poet translator and researcher is the sinologist Stephen Owen (1946–), who has made brilliant achievements.[2] *The Poetry of Meng Jiao and Han Yu*, published in 1975, is the result of his doctoral dissertation. This book not only clarifies the poetry achievements of Meng Jiao and Han Yu, but also puts forward a new perspective on the mid-Tang Dynasty poetry style *Four Tang Poems* (《四唐诗》). Another important book is *The Poetry of the Early Tang*, published in 1977. Owen can be said to be the first person to systematically process the entire *The Poetry of Early Tang Poetry* (《初唐诗》).[3] *The Great Age of Chinese Poetry: High Tang* (《盛唐诗》) published in 1981, *Traditional Chinese Poetry and Poetics* published in 1985, *Late Tang Poetry: 827-860* (《晚唐诗》) and a large number of English-Chinese poems were translated and edited in *An Anthology of Chinese Literature: Beginnings to 1911* in 1996. For the first time, it was placed side by side with the Western classic literature, praised by critics and ordinary Western readers as well. It is also widely used as university textbooks.[4]

Translators of Chinese classical poetry can be generally grouped into

① 朱徽.中国诗歌在英语世界——英美译家汉诗翻译研究 [M].上海：上海外语教育出版社，2009: 85.
② 朱徽.中国诗歌在英语世界——英美译家汉诗翻译研究 [M].上海：上海外语教育出版社，2009: 13.
③ 王洪，田军.唐诗百科大辞典 [M].北京：光明日报出版社，1990: 800.
④ 朱徽.中国诗歌在英语世界——英美译家汉诗翻译研究 [M].上海：上海外语教育出版社，2009: 283-284.

metrical verse school and blank verse school. The first is called as classical school including Herbert Allen Giles, John Turner and Xu Yuanchong, etc. They lay stress on the beauty of sound and form, namely, the rhyme scheme and rhythm pattern of the English version of Chinese classical poetry. British sinologist Herbert Allen Giles insists that verse should be rendered into verse and that rhyme is requisite for rendering the rhymed originals. John Turner points out that the translation of a poem should read like a poem itself, emphasizing the reservation of form and structure. The principle of "three-beauty" and the method of "three-transformation" are regarded as the most important theories of poetry translation by Professor Xu Yuanchong. Especially the principle of three beauty—in sense, sound and form, plays a key role in his series of translation theories. "Three-beauty" is the meeting point of Western aesthetics and Chinese aesthetics to varying degrees. Western aesthetic schools all believe that "formal aesthetics is a holistic concept, because the beauty of form is a holistic, unified structure". Chinese aesthetics also has "imaginary etherealness, inherent reality". In the reality, the overall is a combination of various parts.[1] On the basis of this theoretical common ground, grasping the beauty of the original as a whole is one of the ways to achieve aesthetically fit in translation. In addition, "empathy" in the Western aesthetics is roughly the same as "idea" and is similar to Plato's "inspiration theory", "both emphasizing the active role of subjective emotions, ... greatly enhancing the appeal of poetry".[2] In terms of "beauty", Chinese and Western

---

① 刘宓庆.翻译美学导论 [M]. 北京：中国对外翻译出版公司，2005.

② 顾正阳.古诗词曲英译美学研究 [M]. 上海：上海大学出版社，2006.

aesthetics also attach great importance to the rhythm of poetry, which is also one of the characteristics that distinguish poetry from other styles. The sense is the deep connotation of the poetry, which is usually shown in the way of cultural image, and its rendering determines whether the whole translation is successful or not, while the appropriate manipulation of the sound and form can enhance the beauty in sense.

　　The second is also called as free school, consisting of the translators who render poems in the form of free verse or prose owing to the limitation of metrical form in translation. The representatives include Amy Lowell, Arthur Waley, Witter Bynner, Stephen Owen, and domestic translator Weng Xianliang. They maintain that sticking to the rhyme scheme and rhythm pattern will impair the reproduction in meaning and the mood in translation. Arthur Waley points that the restrictions of rhyme necessarily injure either the vigor of one's language or the literality of one's version, and it is impossible not to sacrifice sense for sound. Professor Weng Xianliang proposes that poetry may be translated into prose. He believes that translators should retain the essence of the original instead of formal similarity. He says, "The translation of a poem is not merely a copy of it. Whether it resembles the original or not, it lies in the spirit, rather than in the appearance. Furthermore, the translation should not be subject to the restraint of original form. It makes no difference whether it is rhymed or divided into lines. It's quite free." ①

---

① 翁显良 . 古诗英译 [M]. 北京 : 北京出版社 , 1985: 18

1.2   Theories of Image Translation

Image is the soul of Chinese classical poetry and plays an exceedingly important role in poetry composition and appreciation. Image is the fusion of the subjective emotion and objective phenomena. Objective phenomena from the outer world can become the creative objects of the poets.

Cultural elements of the image are the soul and focus of poetry translation, especially in culture communication between Chinese and Western countries. Their rich cultural connotations in Tang poetry determine the difficulty of information transmission degree.

Therefore, many scholars hold that the key to the success of poetry translation lies in the manipulation of image, and they try to explore and translate image in poetry from different approaches. For example, Zhang Baohong discusses the reproduction of image in terms of its broad sense and narrow one, Xin Xianyun focuses on the adaptive methods for the translation of image by dividing them into figurative and non-figurative categories, Li Jiaqiang focuses his study on the translation of imagery from the perspective of hermeneutics and reception aesthetics, Jin Ai studies the image transference in Chinese classical poetry from cross-cultural perspective, and Kong Deliang probes into the cultural images in Tang poetry from information theory etc.

Ezra Pound is regarded as the pioneer in the translation of the Chinese classical poetry into English. He tends to reproduce the whole effect of the

10

original poem with half translation and half creation. More importantly, Pound deliberately tries to imitate the form and mood of the original image. However, sometimes he is not willing to or cannot make clear of the hidden information of an image, and he has only to pay attention to the form of it. By doing so, he creates a completely new method of expression—juxtaposition of image. According to Pound's purpose, it is the juxtaposition of image rather than the sense that he should reconstruct in the process of translation. In contrast, Professor Weng Xianliang argues that a translator who cannot betray the original image in translation and reproducing image, which is not just like copying the pictures, is expected to absorb the spirit and essence of the original image. So in rendering image, Professor Weng Xianliang attaches more importance to the poetic feelings of the image and the correct sense behind it. Hence, he is not afraid of giving up the original form of poetry but taking a method of explanation and translating poetry into prose. It can be seen that Ezra Pound generally focuses his attention on the form of image while Weng Xianliang on its sense. Meanwhile, both of them ignore the cultural connotation of image and their translations are usually at the expense of cultural distortion or loss.

As to image rendering in the translation of Chinese classical poetry, Professor Liu Zhongde thinks that a translator may find himself in three situations:

(1) A translator can find expressions which are entirely equivalent to each other;

(2) The translator has to change the imagery;

(3) The translator has to change the surface value of some words so that he may get a suitable representation which can express their true implication.[①]

Accordingly, he proposes four methods of translating image:

(1) Literal translation: it is the most important method in imagery translation;

(2) Transformation: it makes the language vivid and lively though it transforms the original imagery into new ones;

(3) Free translation: it is expected to convey the meaning that the original imagery contains. However, it cannot be overused since it may impair or even lose the imagery and deprive the language of vividness and liveliness;

(4) Transliteration: it is expected to translate imagery phonetically. With lots of difficulties, however, it is seldom used in practice.[②]

Obviously, Liu Zhongde pays great attention to the flavor of cultural image for he puts literal translation as the first method when rendering image since this method can retain the essence of image to the largest extent if possible.

According to Professor Xie Tianzhen, there are three approaches in the discussion of cultural image. The first one is to regard the manipulation of cultural image as a kind of skill, paying much attention to the translation in idioms including proverbs and allusions. It is very useful in giving some

---

① 刘重德. 文学翻译十讲 [M] 北京: 中国对外翻译出版公司, 1991: 23.
② 刘重德. 文学翻译十讲 [M] 北京: 中国对外翻译出版公司, 1991: 95.

practical propositions to the translators. The second one is to discuss the translation of cultural image from the perspective of psychological linguistics. Scholars in this group hold that cultural image in the original works is to give the readers deep impression within the vivid language and its use is to enhance the influence on the readers' inner world. In this sense, translators don't need to transplant all the image in the translation process if their connotation or soul can be expressed in another way. The third one is to discuss image translation based on the cultural perspective. Scholars in this group emphasize that translators must discern the homogeneity and heterogeneity so that they can get the right understanding and transferring of the original image.

1.3   Research Significance

From the above review, two points are made clear of the translation situation of Chinese classical poetry.

The first one is that the translation of Chinese classical poetry is quite fruitful in practice with lots of works and journals published while it is not given scientific and systematic study in theory. Therefore, this translation is expected to be guided by a mature translation theory, and in this sense Equivalence Theory by Eugene Nida is an appropriate choice. It is defined as a translation principle which requires the translator to render the meaning of the original in such a way that the target text will trigger the same impact on the target reader as the original text does upon the original reader. In addition, the form of the target wording is frequently changed according to this theory, but as long as the change follows the rules of back transformation in the source language, of contextual consistency in the rendering process, and of transformation in the receptor language, the message is preserved and so the translation is faithful. Consequently, Nida makes a conclusion that translation consists in reproducing in the receptor language the closest natural equivalent of the source language message, first in terms of meaning, and second in terms of style. Here equivalent cannot be understood in its mathematical meaning of identity, but only in terms of approximation on the basis of degrees of closeness to functional identity. The key concepts of this theory, "closest natural equivalence" and "equivalent effect" , have reasonability, feasibility and popularity in regular translation.

The second one is that it has been agreed generally that cultural image is the soul of Chinese classical poetry and determines the success of its translation. Image may be defined as the representation through language of sensory experience, or the use of figurative language to produce pictures in the mind of readers or hearers. Poetry appeals directly to our senses, of course, through its rhyme and rhythms, which people can actually appreciate when it is read aloud. But indirectly it appeals to our senses through imagery, a mental picture, something seen in the mind's eye. Generally, visual image is the most frequently used in poetry, but an image may also represent a sound, a smell, a taste, a tactile experience (such as hardness or coldness), an internal sensation (such as hunger or nausea).

However, the main study object of this dissertation is cultural imagery. As culture constitutes the context for language communication, more attention are paid to the cultural aspect of the language, and translation becomes a cross-cultural activity. An ideal translation of imagery should be able to integrate both the linguistic meaning and the cultural meaning from the source language to the target language, in order that the Source Language (SL) readers and the Targeted Language (TL) readers can experience the same mind impression and impact.

However, another problem in the translation of Chinese classical poetry exists that it is impossible to study all the ancient poems just in one book. China is one of the earliest countries where poetry originates and also one of the most fruitful ones where poetry develops. Prime Tang period, which extends about 50 years, briefly equals to the ruling period of Emperor Xuanzong, Li Longji (李隆基, 685-762), witnesses the zenith of Chinese classical poetry. Tang Poetry during this period is not only great in quantity, but also extensive in the range of subjects, original in artistry and diverse in forms. The most famous poets during this period and also in Chinese literature history are Li Bai (李白, 701-762) and Du Fu (杜甫, 712-770). Their poems are the epic of Chinese classical poetry and deeply picture the course from prosperity to decline of Tang Dynasty. Li Bai, called "Poet-Immortal", is one of the greatest romantic poets, while Du Fu, remembered as "Poet-Sage", is a realistic poet. Other famous poets such as Meng Haoran (孟浩然, 689-740), Wang Changling (王昌龄, 698-757) and Wang Wei (王维, 701-761) are usually called Pastoral Poets. They pursue moral integrity promoted by Tao Yuanming and embodied by their love of nature and indifference to fame and fortune. Therefore, their poems tend to picture a tranquil and peaceful life or express the ideal of saving the world and benefiting the mankind. In the meantime, Gao Shi (高适, 704-765) and Cen Shen (岑参, 715-770) are called Border Poets. Their poems usually chant the eulogy of heroes or show sympathy for the victims of the wars and revolts. Poetry is life distilled, coming from life and reflecting life. The content of poetry during Prime Tang period almost overlaps with that of Chinese classical poetry as a whole, and ranges from songs depicting the pastoral life to epics recording political upheavals, from describing the harsh living conditions of the lower class to exposing the luxurious ones of the upper class. In the same sense, the theme of poetry during Prime Tang period overlaps with that of Chinese classical poetry as a whole, and ranges from subtle personal emotions to great professional ambitions, from laments for the dead and separation to happiness for the rebirth and reunion, etc.

Based on the above presentation and consideration, this book will focus on the translation of cultural image in Chinese classical poetry during Tang Dynasty especially Prime Tang period in the light of Equivalence Theory.

Chapter 2　The Equivalence Theory of Translation

2.1　Major Presentations of Translational Equivalence

Equivalence is a term used in translation theory to describe the nature and extent of the relationships that exist between SL and TL texts or smaller linguistic units. In poetry translation it basically refers to the equal quality in meaning and mood between the original and translation versions. The precise sense in which translation equivalence is understood varies from person to person. In the history of translation many scholars present the theory of equivalence and make a great contribution to the translation practice.

J. C. Catford proposes, "Translation may be defined as follows: the replacement of textual material in one language (SL) by equivalent textual material in another language (TL)" .[①] He tries to make a distinction between "formal correspondence" and "textual equivalence" . And he maintains

---

① CATFORD J C. A linguistic theory of translation[M]. Oxford: Oxford University Press, 1965:12.

that the central task of translation theory is that of defining the nature and conditions of translation equivalence and the central problem of translation practice is that of finding TL rendition equivalence. In his opinion, the textual equivalence can be quantified and translation equivalence may be achieved at different ranks, suggesting a dynamic understanding of equivalence instead of a static one.

Juliane House proposes her definition of translation as the replacement of a text in the source language by a semantically and pragmatically equivalent text in the target language. She lays emphasis on pragmatic equivalence. In her opinion, it is always necessary to aim at equivalence of pragmatic meaning in translation if necessary at the expense of semantic equivalence. Pragmatic meaning thus overrides semantic meaning. However, in contrast, O. Kade insists that semantic equivalence have great priority in transferring process. And he classifies the potential translation equivalence relation into four categories: total equivalence, optional equivalence, approximate equivalence, and zero equivalence.[1]

In his definition of translation equivalence, Anton Popovic in his article *Translation as Communication* distinguishes four types: ① Linguistic equivalence, where there is homogeneity on the linguistic level of both SL and TL texts, i.e. word for word translation. ② Paradigmatic equivalence, where there is equivalence of "the elements of a paradigmatic expressive axis" , i.e. elements of grammar, which Popovic sees as being a higher

---

① HOUSE J. Translation[M]. Oxford : Oxford University Press, 2009:35

category than lexical equivalence. ③ Stylistic (translational) equivalence, where there is "functional equivalence of elements in both original and translation aiming at an expressive identity with an invariant of identical meaning" . ④ Textual (syntagmatic) equivalence, where there is equivalence of the syntagmatic structuring of a text, i.e. equivalence of form and shape. It can be seen that translation involves far more than replacement of lexical and grammatical items between languages and that the process may involve discarding the basic linguistic elements of the SL text so as to achieve Popovic's goal of "expressive identity" between the SL and TL texts.① But once the translator moves away from close linguistic equivalence, the problems of determining the exact nature of the level of equivalence aimed for begin to emerge. It is an established fact that if a dozen translators tackle the same poem, they will produce a dozen different versions. And yet somewhere in those dozen versions there will be what Popovic calls the "invariant core" of the original poem. This invariant core, he claims, is represented by stable, basic and constant semantic elements in the text.

In trying to solve the problem of translation equivalence, Albrecht Neubert postulates that from the perspective of context, translation equivalence must be considered to be a semiotic category, comprising syntactic, semantic and pragmatic components. These components are arranged in a hierarchical relationship, where semantic equivalence takes

---

① POPOVIC A .Anthology of studies on translation[M].Tel AAviv Edmonton: The University of Alberta, 1980:45−61.

priority over syntactic equivalence, and pragmatic equivalence conditions and modifies both the other elements. Equivalence overall results from the relation between signs themselves, the relationship between signs and what they stand for, and the relationship between signs, what they stand for and those who use them.

All the theories or ideas of translational equivalence presented above have one thing in common: equivalence is the goal or ideal of any translation. However, the above scholars do not give a scientific deliberation or explanation. Consequently, their presentations are lack of persuasiveness to some extent. In contrast, Equivalence Theory by Eugene Nida is much more systematic and recognized as a mature theory in translation. Of course, Nida also uses some of the above presentations for reference to gradually perfect his own theory.

2.2 The Theory of Functional Equivalence by Eugene Nida

2.2.1 Formal Equivalence and Dynamic Equivalence

In his masterpiece *Toward a Science of Translating* in 1964, Eugene Nida distinguishes two types of equivalence, formal and dynamic, where formal equivalence "focus attention on the message itself, in both form and content" . In such a translation one is concerned with such correspondences as poetry to poetry, sentence to sentence, and concept to concept. Eugene Nida calls this type of translation a "gloss translation" , which aims to allow the reader to understand as much of the SL context as possible. Consequently, in formal equivalence the form (syntax and classes of words) is preserved while the meaning is often lost or distorted. Therefore, Nida specially differentiates between meaning and style. He maintains that when one must be abandoned for the sake of the other, the meaning must take priority over the stylistic forms.[1]

Dynamic equivalence is initiated by Eugene Nida in terms of the "closest natural equivalent" , based on the principle of equivalent effect, i.e. that the relationship between receptor and message should aim at being the same as that between the original receptors and the SL message. In the 1980s, Nida restated the theory in *On Translation*, in collaboration with Pro. Jin Ti, as follows: The dynamic character of such translation depends upon a comparison of two relations. That is to say, the relation of the target language receptors to the target language text should be roughly equivalent to the relationship between the original receptors and the original text. It is this double relationship that provides the basis for dynamic equivalence. Based on sociology, psychology, linguistics, semiotics and cultural anthropology, etc, the theory emphasizes not on the simple static equivalence in form of language, but on what a translation does or performs in the interlingual communication. The great contribution Nida has made is to shift the focus from the comparison of a pair of texts, the source language and the target language texts, to a comparison of the two-way communication process involved.

---

① NIDA E. Toward a science of translating[M].Leiden: Brill Academic Publishers, 1964:143.

2.2.2 Functional Equivalence in Translation

In his book *From One Language to Another*, Nida changes the term "dynamic equivalence" into "functional equivalence" without anything changed in essence of the theory. Nida explains that "dynamic equivalence" has been treated in terms of the "closest natural equivalence", but the term has been misunderstood by some persons as referring only to something which has impact. Accordingly, many individuals have been led to think that if a translation has considerable impact then it must be a correct example of dynamic equivalence. Because of this misunderstanding and in order to emphasize the concept of communicative function, it has seemed much more satisfactory to use the expression "functional equivalence" in describing the degrees of adequacy of a translation.

According to Eugene Nida, functional equivalence implies different degrees of adequacy from minimal to maximal effectiveness on the basis of both cognitive and experiential factors. A minimal, realistic definition of functional equivalence can be stated as "the readers of translated text should be able to comprehend it to the point that they can conceive of how the original readers of the text must have understood and appreciated it".① A maximal, ideal definition can be stated as "the readers of a translated text should be able to understand and appreciate it in essentially the same

---

① DE WAARD J, NIDA. From one language to another: functional equivalence in Bible translating[M].Nashville: Thomas Nelson Publishers, 1986: 132.

manner as the original readers did" . [1] The maximal definition implies a high degree of language-culture correspondence between the source and target languages and an unusually effective translation so as to produce in receptors the capacity for a response very close to what the original readers experienced. In the texts involving only routine information, this maximal level of equivalence is attempted to achieve.

It is worth noting that the concept of "receptor" (here used as a synonym of "reader") plays an important part in functional equivalence. According to Eugene Nida, "translating means communicating, and this process depends on what is received by persons hearing or reading a translation" . [2] What is important in judging the validity of a translation, therefore, is the extent to which receptors correctly understand and appreciate the translated text. Accordingly, it is essential that functional equivalence should be stated primarily in terms of a comparison of the way in which the original receptors understand and appreciate the text, and the way in which receptors of the translated text understand and appreciate the translated text. There are a number of fundamental problems involved in studying translation adequacy in terms of "response of readers" , since both determining how the readers of the original text comprehend it and evaluating effectively the responses of those who read a translated text are

---

[1] DE WAARD J, NIDA E. From one language to another: functional equivalence in Bible translating[M].Nashville: Thomas Nelson Publishers, 1986: 151.
[2] DE WAARD J, NIDA E. From one language to another: functional equivalence in Bible translating[M].Nashville: Thomas Nelson Publishers, 1986: 21

equally difficult and even impossible.

Consequently, it is best to speak of "functional equivalence" in terms of a range of adequacy, since no translation is ever completely equivalent. Equivalence cannot be understood in its mathematical meaning of identity, but only in terms of proximity, i. e. on the basis of degrees of closeness to functional identity. As to a translator, the main task is to give full play to his creative power while utilizing all the resources at his command and come to a version which he judges to be the closest approximation to the original. In fact, to achieve a satisfactory functional identity, a translator cannot merely make a compromise between the literal and liberal translation nor can one succeed by merely simplifying the grammar and restricting the number of wording. Therefore the translators have to: ① weigh all the factors involved in the communication; ② produce various alternative renderings; ③ test the acceptability and intelligibility of such rendering with receptors.

Firstly, a functional equivalent translation cannot effectively be achieved unless the translator has a profound understanding of all factors, which shape the meanings and styles of the source and target texts. These factors, which range from the various linguistic and cultural features of the source text to the capacity and motivation of target receptors, and to the circumstances the target text is to be employed, must be all reflected in the target text wording and syntax. Secondly, in a sense the process of transferring is always a matter of choosing the best rendering from different alternatives. The translator had better think out more than one way of reproducing the source text, particularly a complex text, and then select the closest or the most natural one from such ways. Thirdly, a competent translator will try to imagine that the intended receptors are listening to or reading the translation on the spot. Awareness should be raised and efforts should be made in keeping with the acceptability and intelligibility of the potential receptors.

Above all, the key concepts of Equivalence Theory, the closest natural equivalence and equivalent effect, have reasonability and popularity in regular translation and guide the translation process. Simply speaking, the Equivalence Theory in translation is a process of achieving the closest natural equivalence by choosing the most appropriate translation method. The changeable choice in translation method is based on the consideration of all factors in functional identity and is expected to achieve the same effect on the target receptors as the original text does upon the original readers. On the basis of this analogy, Equivalence Theory in the translation of cultural image in fact refers to achieving the closest functional identity of the original imagery by dynamically selecting the most suitable rendering way so that the target text readers have the closest understanding of the original poem.

Chapter 3   Cultural Image and Its Translation from the Perspective of Equivalence Theory

3.1   Cultural Image—the Soul of Classical Poetry

3.1.1   Culture and Image

Ci Hai (《辞海》), a grand dictionary of Chinese language, explains the word "image" like this:

(1) A kind of imaginary form of expression which is reconstructed from memorial phenomenon or conscious shape. It is also called "aesthetic image" in literary creating. The author sublimes the materials which are from real life and experience through imagination, and creates an image in his mind.

(2) A term in Chinese classical literary theory. It refers to a mind which melts subjective affection into an extrinsic image.

Image (Yi Xiang) has long been a central concern of Chinese poetry from its very beginning and first appears in the *Book of Changes* (《易经》), a philosophical work reflecting ancient people's mode of thinking. However, Yi and Xiang remains two separate terms until Liu Xie（刘勰，465–520）proposes them together in his famous *Carving a Dragon with a Literary Mind*（《文心雕龙》）. In the 26th chapter "Spiritual Thinking（神　思）", he says, "The uniquely discerning carpenter wield his ax with his eyes to the imagery（独照之匠，窥意象而运斤）". In his understanding, imagery is the visualization of the composition of literary work, the sensory perception of the physical world—artistic embryo which comes into being by the carrier of language. Hu Yinglin（胡应麟，1551–1602）in Ming Dynasty believes in his *Commentary on Poetry*（《诗薮》）that the charm of ancient Chinese poetry lies in the employment of imagery（古诗之妙，专求意象）. In short, image is an aboriginal notion in Chinese classical poetry theory. In stead of simply seeking objective correlatives of subjective emotions in concrete objects, poets call for a higher level of poetic world in creating image—the concordant combination of explication and implication, a unification of sense and emotion, and a fusion of nature and self.

Language is the carrier of image. Language is the bridge to express poets' emotion and affection. Wang Bi（王弼，226–249）during Jin Dynasty says, "nothing can equal language in giving the fullness of imagery; image is overt in language（尽象莫若言；象以言著）". The relationship between image and culture can be simply considered to be the extension of the relationship between language and culture. As a visible form of cultural content, language is deeply rooted in culture and hence shaped by it. As a system of signs, language has in itself a cultural value. It expresses, embodies and symbolizes cultural reality. Culture always stands with language so that the different image in the language will reflect a certain trait of a certain culture. According to Xie Tianzhen, image is the crystallization of cultural history and wisdom, owing to much contribution of the folklores, worships and tribe's unique totems of different nations. The lengthy evolution of each nation's civilization witnessed frequent appearance of cultural image in language and literary creation of different generations. Thus the image has developed into some symbol, culturally-loaded one, endowed with stable and peculiar cultural connotation, that whenever and wherever the mention of the image will arouse immediate sympathetic responses among people from the same cultural community.[①]

Due to the complexity of cultural image, it is very difficult to give a clear-cut and all-inclusive definition. Cultural image may suggest different meanings in literature, but in spite of their disparities, it is generally accepted to be the representation of sensory experience through language, namely the pictures which we perceive with our senses from the poem. Cultural image will evoke the meaning and truth of human experiences not in the abstract language, but in more perceptible and tangible sensory forms. It is the soul of Chinese classical poetry and plays an exceedingly important role in composition and appreciation. It is the cultural image whose employment makes the poetry vivid and connotative, which is beneficial to understand and appreciate the poetic content and theme, and recaptures the particular social picture to the target readers. It is the

---

① 谢天振.译介学 [M].上海:上海外语教育出版社,1999:180-181.

cultural image embedded with rich cultural associations that attributes to the complexity and charm of poetry, but at the same time it presents the difficulty and confusion in the translation. As culture constitutes the context for language communication, more attention is paid to the cultural aspect of the language, and translation itself is a cross-cultural activity. An ideal translation of image should be able to integrate both the linguistic meaning with the cultural meaning from the source language to the target language, in order that the SL readers and the TL readers can have the same impression and experience the same impact.

3.1.2   Main Characteristics of Cultural Image in Tang Poetry

Planted and flourished in the soil of culture, image bears its unique fragrance in Chinese classical poetry. Earlier in Ming Dynasty, Wang Fuzhi (王夫之, 1619-1692) once systematically explored the four characteristics of image in poetry: integrity, authenticity, ambiguity and originality. In modern times, Professor Peng Jianming holds that the main characteristics of image are derivableness, mouldableness, illusiveness and jumpiness while Professor Wu Sheng proposes such characteristics as subjective individuality, rich symbolism and vagueness. This book will simply put forward two typical features: figurativeness and subjectivity.

1 Figurativeness

The language of poetry is rich in the sense that leaves a lot of open space to the readers' imagination and association. A common approach is to use figurative language, namely, figure of speech, some metaphorical devices such as simile, metaphor, metonymy, personification, etc. Such as a familiar example for the SL readers is *Ode to Willows* (《咏柳》) by He Zhizhang (贺知章, 659−744):

碧玉妆成一树高，

万条垂下绿丝绦。

不知细叶谁裁出，

二月春风似剪刀。

Ten thousand branches of all trees begin to sprout,

They drop like fringes of a robe made of green jade.

Do you know by whom these young leaves are cut out?

The early spring wind is sharp as scissor blade. (Tr. Xu Yuanchong)[①]

There are "碧玉" in the first line, and "剪刀" in the last line. They are similes: the tender green willow buds are compared to green jade and the early spring wind is compared to scissors, implying that the green willow trees begin to sprout almost all of a sudden, like the long and thick hair of a lady.

The second example is *Qiupu Song* (《秋浦歌》) by Li Bai:

白发三千丈，

缘愁似个长。

不知明镜里，

何处得秋霜。

My white hair is thirty thousand feet long!

It is due to deep sorrow that has made it so long.

---

① 许渊冲.唐诗三百首新译 [M].北京：中国对外翻译出版公司，1997:56.

If I were not in this bright mirror, where could I know,

My temples have got so frosty and terribly wrong! (Tr. Tang Yihe)[①]

In the first line there is a hyperbole or exaggeration: the poet exaggerates his hair to extreme length but of course without intending to be true in the real world. In the last line there is a metonymy: he compares his grey hair to frost with deeper impression, which succeeds to air the poet's grievances and resentment against the society.

Another example is the poem *Love Seeds* (《相思》) by Wang Wei:

红豆生南国，

春来发几枝。

愿君多采撷，

此物最相思。

Red berries grow in southern land,

In spring they overload the trees.

Gather them till full is your hand,

They would revive fond memories. (Tr. Xu Yuanchong)[②]

In this poem red berry is a kind of plant symbol to indicate the poet's love to his dear. Symbolism is an important device for poets to represent or extend meanings, especially abstract ones, which are usually difficult to express. Broadly speaking, symbolism can be included into figurative language.

In Du Fu's *Ascending the Yueyang Tower* (《登岳阳楼》):

---

① 唐一鹤. 英译唐诗三百首 [M].天津：天津人民出版社，2005：67.

② 许渊冲. 唐诗三百首新译 [M].北京：中国对外翻译出版公司，1997:81.

昔闻洞庭水，今上岳阳楼。

吴楚东南坼，乾坤日夜浮。

亲朋无一字，老病有孤舟。

戎马关山北，凭轩涕泗流。

I have heard the fame of Lake Dongting long ago,

And now on Yueyang Tower I see the view glow.

Water makes lands of Wu and Chu to the east and south part;

Day and night the sun and moon on the waves floats and start.

From my dear folks and friends there is no message,

I keep to a lonely boat for disease and age,

Northland is under the tribal horses' trample;

My tears drip down on the window of the chamber. (Tr. Wu Juntao)[1]

It is amazing that we get to know Lake Dongting has possessed with the natural power to separate the land of Wu from that of Chu and get the sun and the moon to float there day and night. On the top of that, Yueyang Tower is so imposing that Du Fu can have a bird's view and enjoy a grand and magnificent scenery of Dongting. This is not the exaggeration, but it combines people's vision with their sensation. However, when it is connected with images like boat, war, balustrade and tears, old and ill, a mind of solitude and loneliness springs onto the paper. So the poet's pessimism and homesickness can be felt in the words, and this is also the true portray of his old age's living situation.

---

[1] 许渊冲，陆佩弦，吴钧陶 . 唐诗三百首新译 [M]. 北京：中国对外翻译出版公司，1988: 189.

In Wang Wei's *In the Hills* (《山中》) :

荆溪白石出，天寒红叶稀。

山路元无雨，空翠湿人衣。

White pebbles hear a blue stream glide;

Red leaves are strewn on cold hillside.

Along the path no rain is seen;

My gown is moist with drizzling green. (Tr. Xu Yuanchong)[1]

In Xu Yuanchong's translation, he translated "空翠"into "drizzling green", by using the simile "greenness falls like drizzle" . The target readers receive the information that this experience is not true and will realize the sprinkle will moisten the gown gradually. They will feel the damp air wets their clothes when walking in the woods and the scene goes into their heart further by repeated chant. It is the feeling that makes the readers refreshed and pleased and reaches to the artistic conception produced by the poet.

2 Subjectivity

As an excellent poet, his emotional experiences are not described in the direct way, he blends his true feelings into the concrete objects which are to be described. The poet never chooses the objects at will, on the contrary, he makes choices mainly depending on his keen insight and special aesthetic view. When the external objective objects are endowed with inner subjective feelings, they become the image, the sensory representation of the poetry. Moreover, the same image would bear different feelings when it

---

[1]　许渊冲 . 唐诗三百首新译 [M]. 北京：中国对外翻译出版公司，1997:126.

is employed by different poets with different life background or in different time. For example, the moon is the image appearing most often in Chinese classical poetry. It is often employed to indicate loneliness due to missing the family members, the loved ones or the hometown since it always hangs alone in the sky. Some familiar poems of the moon could be appreciated in this sense such as Li Bai's *Thoughts on a Tranquil Night* (《静夜思》) and *Song of the Moon over Mount E'mei* (《峨眉山月歌》).

床前明月光，

疑是地上霜。

举头望明月，

低头思故乡。

Before my bed a pool of light,

Is it hoarfrost upon the ground?

Eyes raised, I see the moon so bright;

Head bent, in homesickness I'm drowned. (Tr. Xu Yuanchong)[1]

峨眉山月半轮秋，

影入平羌江水流。

夜发清溪向三峡，

思君不见下渝州。

Over Mount E'mei in autumn the half moon was hanging.

Its shadow was reflected on the Pingqiang River when flowing.

I set off at night from Qingxi Stop to the Three Gorges sailing.

---

① 许渊冲，陆佩弦，吴钧陶. 唐诗三百首新译 [M]. 北京：中国对外翻译出版公司，1988: 125.

I missed you but in vain while on journey to Yuzhou drifting. (Tr. Tang Yihe)[1]

However, because of its clarity and lucidity, the moon is also rich in the intension of emotional purity and moral integrity, to state the poet's aspiration or ambition. Such cultural association can be seen from *Birds Twittering in Gully* (《鸟鸣涧》) and *My Mountain Villa in an Autumn Evening* (《山居秋暝》) by Wang Wei:

> 人闲桂花落，
>
> 夜静春山空。
>
> 月出惊山鸟，
>
> 时鸣春涧中。

I hear osmanthus blooms fall unenjoyed；

When night comes, hills dissolve into the void.

The rising moon startles the birds to sing；

Their fitful twitters fill the dale with spring. (Tr. Xu Yuanchong)[2]

This poem describes the pastoral life in seclusion which gives readers an enjoyment of country life. Here the image of moon helps to create calmness and satisfactory mood of the poet.

> 空山新雨后，天气晚来秋。
>
> 明月松间照，清泉石上流。
>
> 竹喧归浣女，莲动下渔舟。
>
> 随意春芳歇，王孙自可留。

① 唐一鹤.英译唐诗三百首[M].天津：天津人民出版社，2005：231.
② 许渊冲.唐诗三百首新译[M].北京：中国对外翻译出版公司，1997:97.

After the rain has bathed the desolate mountain,

The fresh evening air blows the breath of autumn.

Into the forest of pines the moon sheds her light.

Over the glistening rocks the spring water glides.

Bamboo leaves make noise when washer-girls go home;

The moving dories scattered the lotus blooms.

The fragrance of the vernal plants is on the wane;

Despite all this, here is the place I like to remain. (Tr. Wu Juntao)①

After fresh rain in mountain bare,

Autumn permeates evening air.

Among pine trees bright moonbeams peers;

Over crystal stones flows water clear.

Bamboos whisper of washer-maids,

Lotus stirs when fishing boat wades.

Though fragrant spring may pass away,

Still here's the place for you to stay. (Tr. Xu Yuanchong)②

From the above translation versions, a tranquil and beautiful pastoral scenery is emerging, a series of images including the moon and washer-girl unfolding, and carries the calm and noble thoughts and feelings of the poet, the tranquility of his heart, and reminds target readers of the Eden that the poet is looking forward to. The poet's artistic technique is to express his

---

① 许渊冲，陆佩弦，吴钧陶 . 唐诗三百首新译 [M]. 北京：中国对外翻译出版公司，1988: 71.

② 许渊冲 . 唐诗三百首新译 [M]. 北京：中国对外翻译出版公司，1997:102.

unsullied personality and his ideal society through portrayal of the beauty of the great nature.

The lines in Li Bai's *Drinking under the Moonlight* (《月下独酌》) goes in this way:

举杯邀明月，对影成三人。

Raising my cup I beckon the bright moon,

For he, with my shadow, will make three men. (Tr. Arthur Waley) [1]

Till, raising up my cup, I asked the bright moon,

To bring me my shadow and make us three. (Tr. Witter Bynner) [2]

I raise my cup to invite the Moon who blends,

Her light with my shadow and we're three friends.(Tr. Xu Yuanchong)[3]

The moon is often referred to as Chang'e, who is a poetic symbol of women in the classical poetry. For Xu Yuanchong, a classical poetry translator who is well versed in Chinese culture, he translates this sentence as "Her light with my shadow and we are three friends", which conforms to the poetic symbol of women. It can be obviously seen that Waley's translation is also a mistranslation. He renders it into "for he", causing the Western readers to misunderstand the moon in Chinese cultural image. Meanwhile, his mistranslation distorts the feminine image of the moon in the Tang poetry.

---

[1]　WALEY A. A hundred and seventy Chinese poems[M].London: Constable & Co. Ltd., 1918: 118.

[2]　BYNNER W, KIANG K. The jade mountain: a Chinese anthology[M]. New York: Alfred A. Knopf, 1929:59.

[3]　许渊冲 . 唐诗三百首新译 [M]. 北京：中国对外翻译出版公司，1997:354.

From the above analysis, it's concluded that the same image displays different and even opposite connotations because of different emotions of the poets. The individual with subjective ideas brings about the difficulties in the transmission of image since the cultural memories as well as the sediment of ethnic memories lie in the poets' life. The poet's rich psychological experiences and emotions evoking either in the natural world or under the sophisticated human society do claim his or her invisible but actual involvement in the poetry creation. Therefore, the basic acquaintance with the poet's social or cultural background is the premise for correct understanding and appreciating its translation.

3.1.3 Themes of Image Expression in Tang Poetry

During the course of composing a poem, the poet will firstly set its theme, and then some objective substances will be chosen to ornament this theme. Since literary trends and literati's life in different historical period own some similarities, *The 300 Tang Poems* translated by Xu Yuanchong can classify the whole poems into nine categories according to the themes.

(1) Man and nature, which describes natural scenery and communion of man with nature, such as Du Fu's *Happy Rain on a Spring Night* and Zhang Ruoxu's *The Moon over the River on a Spring Night*.

(2) Nature and hope, which depicts the force and beauty of nature, such as moon, rain, clouds, trees and flowers, to express poets' ambition and aspiration, such as He Zhizhang's *The Willow* and Bai Juyi's *Peach Blossoms in the Temple of Great Forest*.

（3）Farewell, which relates the poets' love of their friends and their sorrows of parting, such as Meng Haoran's *Parting from Wang Wei* and Wang Wei's *Seeing Yuan the Second off to the Northwest Frontier.*

（4）Homeland and nostalgia, which shows the poets' love of their family and homeland, such as Li Bai's *Thoughts on a Tranquil Night* and Meng Jiao's *Song of the Parting Son.*

（5）Love, which reflects the lovers' passionate love through an implicit way. For example, Wang Wei's *Love Seeds* and Li Shangyin's *To One Unnamed .*

（6）Historical themes, which are unlike that in the Western epics, such as Liu Yuxi's *The Street of Mansions* and Li Shangyin's *On History.*

（7）Frontier and wars, which express the poets' detesting of wars, respecting heroes and showing sympathy for plebs. For instance, Wang Changling's *On the Frontier* and Lu Lun's *Border Songs.*

（8）Politics and satire, which usually satirizes the corrupt government and muddled society, such as Du Fu's *Song of the Conscripts* and Bai Juyi's *The Old Charcoal Seller*, etc.

（9）Reflections and recollections, which shows poets' achievements or frustration. For instance, Du Fu's *On the Height* and Li Bai's *Drinking Alone Under the Moonlight.*

3.1.4   Classification of Image in Tang Poetry

According to the *The Complete Collection of Tang Poetry* data base, using

ACCESS, data processing tools such as MySQL and PHP. [①]The images in *The Complete Collection of Tang Poetry*:

Names of Image	Number	Percentage
flower	9 398	22%
color	89	0.21%
mountain	942	2.2%
cloud	11 147	26.1%

Hence, the conclusion can be made that poets in the Tang Dynasty like to employ the image most by the description of the clouds and flowers, comparing with those in *The Complete Collection of Song Ci Poetry*, in which the flowers rank first. In Tang and Song periods, flower, mountain and cloud are the typical images.

1 Color as image

In Chinese classical poetry, there are many color images for the poets to create certain scenery or emotion. The poets always utilize the color images, which have abundant culture information. They become the special carrier of poets' inner mind. However, what actually matters is the semantic content of the image, but not the color itself. Take two poems as example: one is the poem *Lodging in Mt. Hibiscus on a Stormy Night* (《逢雪宿芙蓉山主人》) by Liu Changqing, and the other is the last two lines from *A Spring View* (《春望》) by Du Fu.

---

① 蔡爱娟. 基于数据库的唐诗宋词对比研究 [J]. 科技视界，2015(25): 162-163.

日暮苍山远，

天寒白屋贫。

柴门闻犬吠，

风雪夜归人。

The vesper bedims the remote grey hill,

Frigidity reigns over a shabby domicile.

Outside the humble gate travels a barking sound,

From amidst the blizzard a soul's homebound. (Tr. Huang Long)[①]

白头搔更短，

浑欲不胜簪。

I scratch my head, and my grey hair has grown too thin,

It seems, to bear the weight of the jade clasp and pin. (Tr. Wu Juntao)[②]

In the first poem, the images with colors like "苍山" and "白屋" are to describe a cold snow-covered scene together with a poor family to arouse a sad feeling. In the translation, "仓" is properly rendered into the referential meaning "grey" while "白" into associative meaning "shabby". In the second poem, the color image "白头" is a transferred epithet and "白" actually modifies hair but not head, and is properly translated into grey but not white.

Let's examine another example of poem, Li Bai's *Seeing Meng Haoran off at Yellow Crane Tower* (《黄鹤楼送孟浩然之广陵》):

故人西辞黄鹤楼，

---

① 许渊冲，陆佩弦, 吴钧陶. 唐诗三百首新译 [M]. 北京：中国对外翻译出版公司, 1988:180.

② 许渊冲，陆佩弦, 吴钧陶. 唐诗三百首新译 [M]. 北京：中国对外翻译出版公司, 1988:151.

烟花三月下扬州。

孤帆远影碧空尽，

唯见长江天际流。

My friend has left the west where Yellow Crane Tower's,

For Yangzhou in spring green with willows and red with flowers.

His lessening sail is lost in the boundless azure sky,

Where I see nothing but the endless River rolling by. (Tr.Xu Yuanchong)[①]

In this poem, "Yan Hua (烟花)" is a famous and marvelous image, symbolizing the beautiful scenery of spring. In Xu Yuanchong translation, the image is not reproduced in a word-for-word way but in an artistic way. He translates it into green willows and red flowers, which can avoid the superficial obscurity in meaning and acquire the central connotation hidden in the elaborate wording. Moreover, the image of "March" is translated into "spring" to present a beautiful and pleasant seasonal scenery in the readers' imagination, and other images such as "Gu Fan(孤帆)" "Bi Kong(碧空)" "Tian Ji(天际)" are also understood and translated appropriately and successfully. All these help to bring us a vivid parting picture and impart the poet's rich sentiments to his friend and sigh at the transience of human life and the permanency of the universe.

Have a look at Bai Juyi's employment of "green" and "red" in *Asking Liu Shijiu* (《问刘十九》)：

绿蚁新醅酒，红泥小火炉。

---

① 海岸. 中西诗歌翻译百年论集 [C]. 上海：上海外语教育出版社, 2007：11.

A honest rough new wine. A swim in it, green ants of vine. (Tr. Xu Yuanchong)①

My new brew gives green glow. My red clay stove flames up. (Tr. Yuan Xingpei)②

The poet puts two contrasting colors of "green" and "red" in the first couplet, giving people the brightness and briskness. The warm color "red" gives the readers a warm feeling, sensing the atmosphere of home and indicating reunion in the source culture. Without relevant background knowledge, translators find it hard to translate "绿蚁" accurately. Indeed, Xu Yuanchong translation is literally translated as "green ants". Although the color is retained, its meaning is lost completely. Imagine how the green ants swim in the wine. If the incredible scene is transmitted to its target readers, who dares to drink this wine? In the ancient China, wine is made from cooked coriander, sorghum or chestnut. Looking very turbid, there is scum floating on the wine surface, it will be transparent under the light, the glittering green light. Therefore, the translator translates "green ants" in the original poem by preserving its true meaning instead of its surface meaning. Professor Yuan Xingpei translates "绿蚁" into "green glow ". In this way, the image becomes fresh and pleasant, stimulating the reader's strong desire to sip.

In the first two lines in Du Fu's *A Quatrain* (《绝句》) go as follows:

---

① 顾正阳. 古诗词曲英译文化探索 [M]. 上海：上海大学出版社, 2007: 56.
② 袁行霈. 中国文学史 [M]. 北京：高等教育出版社, 1999: 47.

两个黄鹂鸣翠柳，一行白鹭上青天。

Two golden orioles sing amid the willows green;

A flock of white egrets fly into the blue sky. (Tr. Xu Yuanchong) ①

Poet, like a skilled painter, gives us a colorful picture. The scene is white and blue, yellow and green, how bright colors! In translation, golden echoes blue with green and white, neat and succinct. The picture of the white egret flying in lines under the blue sky and white clouds unfolds before our eyes. It sounds as if you can hear orioles sing joyfully. Thinking of this, your mood will also be relaxing.

2 Flower as image

Flower is the embodiment of the truth, kindness and beauty, however, human beings worship and seek the truth, kindness and beauty. Therefore, flower is the eternal theme for the artists throughout human's history. In the west, Shakespeare compared beauty to the flowers in April in his Sonnet. Connotation of flowers extends to the quality of truth and kindness people long for. But types of the flowers are diverse from those in China, such as sweet basil, daisy, bellflower, anemone, rumex etc. They have been endowed with different cultural beauty and spiritual beauty. Flower plays an important part in Tang poetry, especially peony, lotus and chrysanthemum are even more numerous. Images of flowers are in Tang poems: any flower, experiencing its blooming, withering, and bearing fruits. All of these touch the poet's nerves and feelings. Flower in bloom will inspire poet's love

---

① 许渊冲.唐诗三百首新译 [M].北京：中国对外翻译出版公司，1997:113.

for life, while withered flowers will evoke the poet about life passing and flowing sigh. Sometimes because of some life encounters, flowers will also trigger poets' different life perception.

（1）Expressing joy and leisure by flowers.

In Du Fu's *Happy Rain on a Spring Night*（《春夜喜雨》）:

好雨知时节，当春乃发生。

随风潜入夜，润物细无声。

野径云俱黑，江船火独明。

晓看红湿处，花重锦官城。

Good rain knows its time right,

It will fall when comes spring.

With wind it steals in night,

Mute, it wets everything.

Over wild lanes dark cloud spreads;

In boat a lantern looms,

Dawn sees saturated reds;

The town's heavy with blooms. (Tr. Xu Yuanchong)①

A good rain knows its season,

And comes when spring is here.

On the heels of the wind it slips secretly into the night,

Silent and soft.

---

① 许渊冲 . 文学与翻译 [M]. 北京: 北京大学出版社，2003: 85

It moistens everything low clouds hang black above the country roads,

A lone boat on the river sheds a glimmer of light.

At dawn we shall see splashes of rain—washed red,

Drenched, blooms in the City of Brocade. (Tr. Yang Xianyi, and Gladys Yang)①

At that time, there was a disaster of drought in the City of Brocade. When the spring rain came, Du Fu couldn't conceal that he was very excited. It came in time and nourished all things. Although the poet's life was in the corner, his patriotism, loyalty and care for people's livelihood would not be changed. From Xu yuanchong's and Yang Xianyi's versions, we feel the tone of the poem is elated and happy. They are faithful to the original. Whether "saturated red" or "washed red", it signifies that flowers bloom after being baptized with rain, which makes the poet ignore the hardships of peripatetic life. On the contrary, it shows the poet's hope about the life.

Another example lies in Meng Jiao's *Successful at the Civil Service Examination* (《登科后》).

昔日龌龊不足夸，今朝放荡思无涯。

春风得意马蹄疾，一日看尽长安花。

Gone are all my past woes! What more have I to say?

My body and my mind enjoy their fill today.

Successful, faster runs my horse in vernal breeze;

I've seen within one day all flowers on the trees. (Tr. Xu Yuanchong)②

① 赵娟.唐诗英译研究 [M].成都：西南财经大学出版社，2018:12.

② 许渊冲.唐诗三百首新译 [M].北京：中国对外翻译出版公司，1997: 201.

Meng Jiao was successful at the civil service examination at the age of 46, that is, he reached success late in life. So he blurted out "successful, faster runs my horse in vernal breeze; I've seen within one day all flowers on the trees." He felt joyful, so all the things in his eyes were beautiful and sweet. All the flowers represented the prosperity of the world was coming in the future, which he thought was promising. Xu Yuanchong's version reflected the poet's high spirit and light mood truthfully.

Look at Han Yu's *Spring Snow* (《春雪》).

新年都未有芳华，二月初惊见草芽。

白雪却嫌春色晚，故穿庭树作飞花。

The new year has yet no fragrant blossoms,

But the second moon suddenly sees the grass sprouting;

The white snow, vexed by the late coming of spring's colors.

Of set purpose darts among the courtyard's trees to fashion flying petals. (Tr. Wen Shu) [1]

On vernal day no flowers were in bloom, alas!

In second moon I'm glad to see the budding grass.

But white snow dislikes the late coming vernal breeze,

It plays the parting flowers flying through the trees. (Tr. Xu Yuanchong)[2]

In English, the nominal vocabulary of flowers is converted into verb,

---

[1]　文殊．诗词英译选 [M] 北京：外语教学与研究出版社，1989: 78.

[2]　许渊冲．唐诗三百首新译 [M].北京：中国对外翻译出版公司，1997: 165.

such as blossom and flower, which work as noun as well as verb. In Wen Shu's and Xu Yuanchong's versions, in order to reflect its dynamic beauty and vitality of the nature, they employed its verbs' −ing forms (progressive tense), sprouting and budding, instead of nouns in the original poem. Meanwhile, it embodies the poet's happy and aggressive spirit. "White snow dislikes the late coming vernal breeze" is similar to Shelly's famous verse "If the winter comes, will the spring be far behind? " in the semantic layer.

(2) Expressing the confusion about life by flowers.

In the first line of Li Bai's *Drinking Alone Under the Moonlight* (《月下独酌》):

花间一壶酒，独酌无相亲。

A cup of wine, under the flowering trees;

I drink alone, for no friend is near. (Tr. Arthur Waley)[1]

From a pot of wine among the flowers,

I drank alone. There was no one with me. (Tr. Witter Bynner)[2]

Whether Bynner's version or Waley's, the poet's sense of isolation in wandering about ideal and reality is placed on the flowers, which accompany the poet to drink. These lines are expressing this feeling to the target readers exactly.

In Liu Xiyi's *Admonition on the Part of a White-haired Old Man* (《代悲白头翁》):

---

[1] Waley A.A hundred and seventy Chinese poems[M].London: Constable & Co. Ltd., 1918: 118.
[2] BYNNER, KIANG K. The jade mountain: a Chinese anthology[M]. New York: Alfred A. Knopf,1929:59.

洛阳城东桃李花，飞来飞去落谁家？

The peach and plum flowers east of the capital,

Fly up and down and here and there. Where will they fall?

年年岁岁花相似，岁岁年年人不同。

The flowers of this year look like those of last year;

But next year the same people will not reappear.(Tr. Xu Yuanchong)[1]

And Cui Hu's poem *Written in a Village South of the Capital* (《题都城南庄》)：

去年今日此门中，人面桃花相映红。

人面不知何处去，桃花依旧笑春风。

In this house on this day last year a pink face vied,

In beauty with the pink peach blossom side by side.

I do not know today where the pink face has gone;

In vernal breeze still smile pink peach blossoms full blown. (Tr. Xu Yuanchong) [2]

From the above two poems, peach blossoms and plum flowers represent the good things, including the youth, the beauty and the loved in the Chinese culture. These two poets strike a similar chord and lament that good things are fleeting and never coming back over time. Hence, the image of flower is the first and foremost choice they make.

(3) Expressing sentiment of parting by flowers.

There was a group of poets in Tang Dynasty, who went through suffering and sorrow caused by ups and downs in the imperial court, such

---

[1]　许渊冲.唐诗三百首新译 [M].北京：中国对外翻译出版公司，1997:153.

[2]　许渊冲.唐诗三百首新译 [M].北京：中国对外翻译出版公司，1997:143.

as "on night by riverside I bade a friend goodbye; in maple leaves and rushes autumn seemed to sigh" in Bai Juyi's *Song of Pipa Player* (《琵琶行》). From the poet's situation, he was exiled by the Emperor. the implication of both maple leaves and rushes is in conformity with the poet's sad mood when he was parting with friend. It is rare that it gathers the maple leaves with rushes in the Tang Poetry. Its rendering gets the parting atmosphere heavy, expressing the poet's grievances for what he experienced in the imperial court.

(4) Expressing the pursuit of lofty character by flowers.

As early as in Warring States period, people associated the flowers with the characters of people. The scent of orchid and osmanthus blossom is the goal of life and ideal state that people are pursuing. Till the Tang Dynasty, flowers, such as peony, lotus, chrysanthemum and plum, are still the soul of poetry and become the incarnation of quality and spirit of the Chinese literati, realizing the perfect combination of flowers and people. From the subject of the talk of Tao Yuanming through Yuan Zhen's "Not that I favor partially the chrysanthemum, but it is the last flower after which none will bloom" to Cen Shen's "Chrysanthemum of my homeland should blow, to beautify the far-off battleground" , they not only praise the high purity of chrysanthemum, but also pin the feelings of concern for the country and the people. Because peony appears not only in the poems but also in painting, it undoubtedly deserves the title of the national flower of the Tang Dynasty. The famous poem concerning peony is seen in Bai Juyi's *Buying Flower* (《买花》) , the acute contrast between the rich who buy peony and the poor who pay taxes. The verses which are vivid to depict the poet's hatred of the ruling class and sympathy to the grass roots are "peonies are at their best hours and people rush to buy the flowers" and "a bunch of deep-red peonies and costs taxes of ten families" respectively. Lotus symbolizes the noble character among the flowers. According to statistics, there are more than three thousand poems concerning lotus since Qu Yuan. It also accounts for a large proportion in the Tang period. In Lu Guimeng's *White Lotus* (《白莲》):

> 素蘤多蒙别艳欺,
>
> 此花端合在瑶池。
>
> 无情有恨何人觉,
>
> 月晓风清欲堕时。

White lotus blooms are often outweighed by red flowers,

They'd rather be transplanted before lunar bowers.

Heartless they seem, but they have deep grief no one knows,

See them fall in moonlight when the morning wind blows. (Tr. Xu Yuanchong) [1]

In this poem, Lu Guimeng does not focus on the white lotus' color and its shape detailedly and directly. On the contrary, he describes the pure spirit of the white lotus blooms: they aren't on a par with showy flowers, and live in the lunar bowers, which is similar with the lotus in Zhou Dunyi's famous lines "how stainless it rises from slimy bed! How modestly it reposes on the clear pool" . With the help of the white lotus, it voices the

---

① 许渊冲 . 唐诗三百首新译 [M]. 北京： 中国对外翻译出版公司 , 1997:203.

grief for the poet's talent remaining unrecognized and his indulging in the state of being self-absorbed.

3 Cloud as image

The ancient Chinese poets raised their heads and looked at the sky and were marveled at the magnificence of the nature. Now, when we read these verses written by the poets centuries ago, people attempt to comprehend the inner meaning hidden behind them. In the sky, clouds have thousands of changes, thus creating all kinds of clouds in poets' works. Among them, more than titles of 50 poems are concerned with clouds. The image of cloud is used in numerous poems. According to data supported by ACCESS, cloud is the image which ranks first, almost 26.1%, in *The Complete Collection of Tang Poetry*, we can't help thinking about cloud from the perspective of cultural connotation. Roughly, cloud is to be split into three categories.

(1) Cloud in the nature.

Considering the cultural gap between China and the West, Chinese way of thinking lacks attention to the feature in naming and classification made the ancient Chinese poets' understanding of cloud, concrete and profound enough, and is still on the perceptual and intuitive layer, such as solitary clouds, twilight clouds, red clouds, yellow clouds, floating clouds, and morning clouds, etc.

For example, in Zu Yong's *Snow Atop the Southern Mountains* (《终南望余雪》):

终南阴岭秀，积雪浮云端。

林表明霁色，城中增暮寒。

How fair the gloomy mountainside!

Snow-crowned peaks float above the cloud.

The forest's bright in sunset dyed,

With evening cold the town's overflowed. (Tr. Xu Yuanchong)[①]

In Gao Shi's famous poems, *Farewell to A Lutist* (《别董大》):

千里黄云白日曛，北风吹雁雪纷纷。

莫愁前路无知己，天下谁人不识君。

Yellow clouds spread for miles and miles have veiled the day;

The north wind blows down snow and wild geese fly away.

Fear not you've no admirers as you go along,

There's no connoisseur on earth but loves your song. (Tr. Xu Yuanchong)[②]

And also in Bai Juyi's *The White Cloud Fountain* (《白云泉》):

天平山上白云泉，云自无心水自闲。

何必奔冲山下去，更添波浪向人间。

Behold the White Cloud Fountain on the Sky-blue Mountain!

White clouds enjoy pleasure while water enjoys leisure.

Why should the torrent dash down from the mountain high.

And overflow the human world with waves far and nigh? (Tr. Xu Yuanchong)[③]

From the above examples, the clouds mentioned in Tang poetry mainly come from the patterns or the colors of clouds, the most intuitive perceptual feature of Chinese people.

---

① 许渊冲.唐诗三百首新译 [M].北京：中国对外翻译出版公司，1997:173.

② 许渊冲.唐诗三百首新译 [M].北京：中国对外翻译出版公司，1997:269.

③ 许渊冲.唐诗三百首新译 [M].北京：中国对外翻译出版公司，1997:132.

（2）Cloud with emotions.

As far as poetry creation is concerned, Sartre holds "one of the main motives of artistic creation is, of course, to feel the relationship between others and the outside world. That is our essence" .[1]The image of cloud is widely used in poetry, which is not only related to the poets' eyes and mind, but also to their spirit and language habit. All things in the nature are sentimental, expressing one's calm and leisure mood by the means of the mountains, rivers and white clouds, which can be seen in Wang Wei's *At Parting*（《送别》）:

下马饮君酒，问君何所之。

君言不得意，归卧南山陲。

但去莫复问，白云无尽时。

Dismounted, I drink with you,

And ask what you've in view.

"I can't do what I will;

So I'll do what I will;

I'll ask you no more, friend,

Let clouds drift without end!" (Tr. Xu Yuanchong) [2]

I dismount from my horse and I offer you wine,

And I ask you where you are going and why.

And you answer: "I am discontent

---

① 陈丹玉.从唐诗中的"云"意象看中国人的自然审美意识 [J].鸡西大学学报, 2015(9):106−110.

② 许渊冲.唐诗三百首新译 [M].北京: 中国对外翻译出版公司, 1997: 362.

And would rest at the foot of the southern mountain.

So give me leave and ask me no questions.

White clouds pass there without end." (Tr. Witter Bynner) [1]

From two versions of this poem, it's obvious that the poet speaks of his love of freedom when parting with his friend, like white clouds drifting without any restraint in the sky.

In Lai Hu's *To the Cloud* (《云》) :

千形万象竟还空，映水藏山片复重。

无限旱苗枯欲尽，悠悠闲处作奇峰。

You have a thousand shapes in flakes or piles in vain;

Hidden in the mountains or on the water you remain.

The drought is so severe that all seedlings would die.

Why won't you come down but leisurely tower high? (Tr. Xu Yuanchong)[2]

On the surface, the poet grumbles that clouds can not be transformed into rain to combat the drought. Acreages of seedlings yearn for the rain eagerly, while the clouds develop into different shapes. In fact, cloud is an oblique reference to the upper classes in the feudal society, who don't care for the hardships people who suffer from at the bottom of the society.

(3) Cloud with Buddhism.

Cloud floats leisurely in the sky and has common with Buddhist monk's

---

[1] BYNNER, KIANG K. The jade mountain: a Chinese anthology[M]. New York: Alfred A. Knopf, 1929: 95.

[2] 许渊冲 . 唐诗三百首新译 [M]. 北京 : 中国对外翻译出版公司 , 1997: 362.

mind, which is in pursuit of freedom persistently. Therefore, Buddhist monk often use cloud to explain the essence of Buddhism. For example, Wang Wei's *Mount Chung-Nan*(《终南山》):

> 太乙近天都，连山接海隅。
>
> 白云回望合，青霭入看无。
>
> 分野中峰变，阴晴众壑殊。
>
> 欲投人处宿，隔水问樵夫。

Its massive height near the City of Heaven,

Joins a thousand mountains to the corner of the sea.

Clouds, when I look back, close behind me,

Mists, when I enter them, are gone.

A central peak divides the wilds,

And weather into many valleys.

Needing a place to spend the night,

I call to a wood−cutter over the river. (Tr. Witter Bynner)[1]

In this poem, the clouds, along with the mists, put on the changeable veil of Zhongnan Mountain. However, the poet enters the mountain, all have disappeared.

It's emptiness that is the essence of Buddhism. It's also reflected in Bai Juyi's *A Flower in the Haze*(《花非花》):

> 花非花，雾非雾。
>
> 夜半来，天明去。

---

[1] BYNNER, KIANG K. The jade mountain: a Chinese anthology[M]. New York: Alfred A. Knopf, 1929: 134.

来如春梦几多时?

去似朝云无觅处。

It looks like a flower, but it isn't a flower;

It looks like fog, but isn't fog.

At midnight it comes about;

It goes away at daybreak,

It comes like a spring dream,

How long can it stay?

And it goes away, no where to find,

Like the morning cloud. (Tr. Tang Yihe)[1]

In this poem, flower is neither the flower nor the fog in the physical form. It seems like the spring dream, while it floats like the morning cloud. Everything and anything in the universe is fleeting, if not illusory, and becomes empty eventually. It is a immaterial and supernatural void in Dhyana.

4 Mountain as image

The famous painter Huang Binhong thinks "the land of China is not beautiful without mountains". There are majestic mountains and hills with little fame spreading all over China. They are in different shapes and feast to our eyes, which attract the literati and poets of the ancient and modern China. They express their feelings by the poems of the mountains. Of course, the image of mountain is an integral part of it. Especially, in

---

① 唐一鹤.英译唐诗三百首 [M]天津:天津人民出版社, 2000: 208.

Tang Dynasty, the poems of mountain become prosperous and is superior in numbers. It is because of the well-off society during that period that poets have enough time and interest to enjoy the beauty of mountains and rivers. Each country has its own mountain cultures. In China, mountains are always used in all kinds of literature works to praise the noble people or unchangeable relationship. However, in Judaism, mountain symbolizes the emergence and arrival of God. Mountains are the icons of people who are noble and conceited, ending up being controlled by the Supreme God.

According to Professor Gu Zhengyang, the mountain images in poems are to be split into four types: mountain for holiness, mountain for eternity, mountain for separation, and mountain for hermit. [1]

(1) Mountain for holiness.

Mountains for holiness in the Tang Poems include two parts: mountains that relate to the religions; mountains that relate to the legends in ancient China. In China, the most important religions are Buddhism and Taoism. Mountains are the objects they love, so a host of mountain images are used in poems concerned with religions. The poets such as Wang Wei, Liu Yuxi, Liu Zongyuan and so on tend to believe in Buddhism and in their work we can see the traces of religion. In their poems, mountains are stable, empty and full of implications; these featuresassemble the themes of Buddhism, conforming to the ideas of some poets who had a grudge against the society. Hence, mountains are the largest space, the symbol of pure nature and

---

① 顾正阳.古诗词曲英译文化溯源[M].北京:国防工业出版社,2010: 99-156.

represent permanence, harmony and aloofness.

In Wang Wei's *The Deerpark Village* (《鹿柴》) :

空山不见人，但闻人语响。

返景入深林，复照青苔上。

No Man is seen in the lonely hills around here,

But whence is wafted the human voice I hear?

So deep in the forest the sunset glow can cross,

That it seems to choose to linger on moss. (Tr. Wu Juntao) [①]

Known as Buddha of poem, Wang Wei who had learned the Buddhism and had achieved the level of calm as emptiness used the image of empty mountain to express the feeling that all is meaningless and only the nature is real, and also his hatred of the official circles and passion for nature . As the target reader knows little about Buddhism or the character of Wang Wei's poems, the translator has to explain the meaning of the image and let them get the meaning and feeling of the poem directly. So the feeling of the image is projected into the translation "空山" into "lonely hills" . In this translation, it's apparent that people feel the situation of the mountain is alone and without company. So it is the poet who was alone in a mountain with nobody else.

Liu Yuxi's well-known saying is that "The mountain will be famous if there are gods in it, not for its height; the river will be famous if there are immortals in it, not for its deepness" . From this, it is not hard to get

---

① 许渊冲，陆佩弦，吴钧陶 . 唐诗三百首新译 [M]. 北京：中国对外翻译出版公司，1988:244.

ancient people to think that mountains are where the immortals live and are wreathed in fairyism. There are great numbers of legends about mountains and they are very well-known among Chinese people, most Chinese people could tell some legends, such as "the monkey enjoying the sea view" and "the immortals basking the boots" in Mount Huang; "Chen Xiang splitting the mountain to save his mother", "playing Xiao to attract phoenix" in Mount Hua; and so on. There are a lot of poems about goddesses and some mountains are thought to be the living place of them.

In Li Bai's *Plain Tune*(《清平调》):

> 云想衣裳花想容，春风拂槛露华浓。
>
> 若非群玉山头见，会向瑶台月下逢。

Her face is seen in flower and her dress in cloud,

A beauty by the rails caressed by vernal breeze,

If not a fairy queen from Jade-Green Mountain proud,

She's Goddess of the Moon in Crystal Hall one sees.(Tr. Xu Yuanchong)[1]

Here, the poet compares Yang Yuhuan to goddess to praise her beauty, fair as a flower, and Mount Jade-Green or Crystal Hall is thought to be the place where Goddess of Moon or Fairy Queen lives, who is the highest goddess in Chinese legends with great power. The target readers could understand how fair Yang Yuhuan is by the means of imagining Goddess of Moon or Fairy Queen.

(2) Mountain for eternity.

When we read the poems that relate to the mountain images, we will

---

[1] 许渊冲.唐诗三百首新译 [M].北京:中国对外翻译出版公司,1997:211.

find out that the words " 江 山 " appears in many times and in those cases the poets do not describe one mountain but refer it to the country, so they become pronoun as the regime. In Tang Dynasty, Li Bai and Du Fu are the representations of poets who write such poems. They were in deep love with their country and they could do something for it, so their poems are filled with a sense of patriotism. It's the magnificence of the mountains that makes people associate them with country. Mountains exist since the very ancient time and they just stay there without any change but the country changes from time to time. The rulers dream that their countries would be as stable as mountains, but it is not easy to achieve.

In Du Fu's *A Quatrain* (《绝句》):

两个黄鹂鸣翠柳，一行白鹭上青天。

窗含西岭千秋雪，门泊东吴万里船。

Two golden orioles sing amid the willows green;

A flock of white egrets fly into the blue sky.

My window frames the snow-crowned western mountain scene;

My door oft sends off junks from far-off Dongwu. (Tr. Xu Yuanchong)[1]

The poet displays a picture: orioles sing gently on the top of green willow; a flock of egrets fly straight to the blue sky; the snow-crowned western mountain is inlaid in my window frame; there is a boat sailing to the far Dong wu at the door of my home. In the translated version, Professor Xu avoids the concept of time, and deftly utilize the vision "the snow-crowned western mountain". What the translator's purpose is to make the

---

[1]　许渊冲.唐诗三百首新译 [M].北京：中国对外翻译出版公司，1997:321.

target readers produce an association successfully: western mountain's peak is covered with snow eternally, which is hard to melt, betokening the regime's never changing.

For the people from all the countries, they hope that their love will last forever. From *The Book of Songs*, poets began to eulogize love and love is an eternal theme for the poetry from generation to generation. There are a lot of poems on love in Tang Poems. In them, mountains are the pronoun of the eternal love as mountains and rivers are the most eternal in the world. Everyone hopes that their love will be as firm and stable as the mountains and never change. In Chinese, the "mountainous vow" fully demonstrates people's wish.

In Yuan Zhen's *Thinking of My Dear Departed*(《离思》):

曾经沧海难为水，除却巫山不是云。

取次花丛懒回顾，半缘修道半缘君。

No water's wide enough when you have crossed the sea;

No cloud is beautiful but that which crowns the peak.

I pass by flowers which fail to attract poor me,

Half for your sake and half for Taoism I seek. (Tr. Xu Yuanchong)[1]

In the original poem, the poet expresses his reminiscence for late beloved wife by "沧海水" and "巫山" whose magnificence symbolize his great affection for his wife when she was alive. In fact, a legend is used. The story was about Chuxiang King who missed a fairy maiden so much that his

---

① 许渊冲. 唐诗三百首新译 [M]. 北京：中国对外翻译出版公司，1997:345.

intestines were broken and the fairy maiden lived in Wu Shan. Professor Xu omits the image "巫山" in his translation instead of "which crowns the peak". In this way, the target readers who lack the cultural background could also feel the same as the poet.

（3）Mountain for separation.

In China, some words and expressions about the ruggedness of the mountains, such as "束马悬车""蚕丛鸟道" etc., exist in our mind. So, to use mountains to express the sadness of departing by the mountain will make it denser, sadder and more grievous. When the readers read the departing of two lovers, they will feel the sorrowful beauty of the poem. The cultural significance of mountains images is to stimulate the aesthetic feelings of the readers under the circumstances of poetry.

For example, the last part in Zhang Ruoxu's *The Moon over the River on a Spring Night* (《春江花月夜》):

斜月沉沉藏海雾，碣石潇湘无限路。

不知乘月几人归，落月摇情满江树。

In the mist on the sea the slanting moon will hide,

It'a long way from the northern hills to southern streams.

How many can go home by moonlight on the tide?

The setting moon shedso'er riverside trees but dreams. (Tr. Xu Yuanchong)[1]

Here "碣石" is the name of a mountain, and "潇湘" is the name of a river.

---

① 许渊冲. 唐诗三百首新译 [M]. 北京：中国对外翻译出版公司，1997: 2.

The author uses these two images to show the long distance and it is not easy to get there. "碣石", the mountain locating in the north, and "潇湘", the river in the south, the translator can bear in mind that the sense of distance should be kept.

In Li Bai's *To the Tune of Pusaman* (《菩萨蛮》):

平林漠漠烟如织，寒山一带伤心碧。

暝色入高楼，有人楼上愁。

玉阶空伫立，宿鸟归飞急。

何处是归程？长亭连短亭。

A flat-top forest stretches far in embroidered mist;

A cluster of mountains cool tinged with heartbreak blue.

The mansion is creeping dusk is clad,

Someone up there is sad.

On marble steps I stand forlorn.

Birds fly hurriedly by back to roost.

Where, pray, is the way home?

Along a string of wayside pavilions I roam. (Tr. Xu Yuanchong)[①]

In Xu Yuanchong's translation, "a cluster of mountains" with "heartbreak blue" makes the English readers feel depressed. The way to hometown is hampered by a cluster of mountains. In particular, "碧" is translated into "blue" by foreignization making people in the background of Western culture sad and also the feeling of separation denser.

This kind of culture may be difficult for the target readers to feel and

---

① 许渊冲.唐诗三百首新译 [M].北京：中国对外翻译出版公司，1997: 255.

understand, therefore, in the translation of such poems, the translators have to show the sorrowful beauty and the relationship between mountains and separation suffering.

(4) Mountain for hermit.

In Chinese history there were a good number of hermits living in the mountains, such as Tao Hongjing living in Mount Juqu and Tao Yuanming in Southern mountain, and so on. They create the rich and colorful Chinese hermit culture. As they live among the mountains and rivers, they could enjoy the beauty of the nature at their leisure, and when they think of their misery life, they tend to write scenery poems to express their feelings and thoughts which make the prosperity of the scenery poetry. In their verses, mountain is no longer a geographical concept but an artistic image containing seclusion or a carrier. There is no earthly clamor, no temptation of fame and wealth, no complicated interpersonal relationship, no bureaucratic strife. They can be lost in beauty of the nature. Such as Tao Yuanming's famous lines "I pluck chrysanthemums under the eastern hedge, and gaze after towards the southern mountains". (Wen Shu, 1989) Therefore, the southern mountain becomes a synonym to signify the sunshine, the comfort and the seclusion among SL readers as well as TL readers.

Look at Bai Juyi's *The White Cloud Fountain* (《白云泉》) again :

Behold the White Cloud Fountain on the Sky-blue Mountain !

White clouds enjoy free pleasure while water enjoys leisure.

Why should the torrent dash down from the mountain high,

And overflow the human world with waves far and nigh? (Tr. Xu Yuanchong)[1]

Professor Xu translates "太平山" into "Sky-blue Mountain". Blue is a cold tone, the match between white and blue indicates the peace and quietness in life. Under such a quiet and harmonious surrounding, even the English readers can't bear to leave such a wonderful seclusion.

In Wang Wei's *Answering Vice-Prefect Zhang* (《酬张少府》):

晚年唯好静，万事不关心。

自顾无长策，空知返旧林。

松风吹解带，山月照弹琴。

君问穷通理，渔歌入浦深。

As the years go by, give me but peace,

Freedom from ten thousand matters.

I ask myself and always answer:

What can be better than coming home?

A wind from the pine-trees blows my sash,

And my lute is bright with the mountain moon.

You ask me about good and evil fortune?...

Hark, on the lake there's a fisherman singing! (Tr. Xu Yuanchong)[2]

After reading it, it's comfortable and blissful that the breeze from the pine trees blows and undress the poet, the moon shining brightly, the poet playing the lute. The poet lauds the seclusion life at his old age, without any worries from bureaucratic strife, which people are longing for.

---

① 许渊冲. 唐诗三百首新译 [M]. 北京: 中国对外翻译出版公司, 1997: 162.

② 许渊冲. 唐诗三百首新译 [M]. 北京: 中国对外翻译出版公司, 1988: 277.

3.2   Semantic Equivalence of Cultural Image

The chief purpose of translation is to convert the meaning of the source language into that of the target language, so the first and foremost task of a translator is to define the meaning of the words or sentences. According to Eugene Nida's statement "Translation consists in reproducing in the receptor language the closest natural equivalent of the source language message, first in terms of meaning and secondly in terms of style. When one must be abandoned for the sake of the other, the meaning must have priority over the stylistic forms." [1] If the translator wants the readers to comprehend the connotation of the image and sense the artistic beauty, first of all the readers must grasp the meaning of the image. Therefore, the first principle for the transference of the image is semantic equivalence, the most essential linguistic equivalence, for semantics is the study of meaning. Clearly it requires that the TL text should evoke similar, if not the same, resonance among the targeted readers stimulated by the original text at the semantic range, namely, the scope of meaning.

In most cases, the meaning of cultural image is multi-layered, consisting of referential meaning and associative meaning. Referential meaning is what an image refers to in the objective world while associative meaning is what the readers can associate it with when they meet it in

---

① NIDA E A. Language and culture: contexts in translating[M]. Shanghai: Shanghai Foreign Language Education Press, 2004: 12.

reading process. Some scholars differentiate the meaning into denotation and connotation. The semantic equivalence of image translation lies in the equivalence in the two layers of meaning, especially the associative or implied meaning. Otherwise, the translation will make no sense. Professor Liu Zhongde argues that without the correct understanding of original text, loyalty to the translation can't be achieved. Regardless of the internal relations in the text, the bad translation mechanically sticks to the literal meaning of isolated words.

Take the lines in *Starting for the Front* (《凉州词》) by Wang Han（王翰, 687—735）for example：

醉卧沙场君莫笑，

古来征战几人回?

Why laugh when they fall asleep drunk on the sand?

How many soldiers ever come home? (Tr. Witter Bynner)[1]

Don't laugh when we lay drunken on the battle ground!

How many warriors ever come back safe and sound? (Tr. Xu Yuanchong)[2]

The image "沙场" originally refers to "a stretch of sands", but it is usually used to imply "battlefield" or "frontier" and its relation to "sand" has gradually disappeared. Therefore, it is not acceptable to translate it directly into "sand" as by Witter Bynner, and Professor Xu's translation is

---

[1] BYNNER W, KIANG K H. The jade mountain: a Chinese anthology[M]. New York: Alfred A. Knopf, 1929: 17.

[2] 许渊冲. 唐诗三百首新译 [M]. 北京：中国对外翻译出版公司，1988: 22.

more reasonable based on correct understanding of the semantic meaning of the image.

Zhang Bi's two lines as an example in his *To Someone in Dream* (《寄人》):

多情只有春庭月，犹为离人照落花

Only the sympathetic moon was shining there.

O'er fallen petals melting like you into the shade. (Tr. Xu Yuanchong)[1]

Xu Yuanchong's translation is like a dynamic montage, creating an empty, sad atmosphere. Ezra Pound has such a similar image "petals on a wet, black bough, the apparition of these faces in the crowd". Pound's rich oriental tone blends Chinese painting with Western culture. Painting-like oriental images are familiar to Western readers. Xu Yuanchong's translation also used "petals" to stroke one's face gently; besides, he added "melting you into" (gradually into), all these creating a kind of moonlight beauty vividly. Scattered petals and dying beauty slowly disappear in the moonlight. Passing away … These superimposed, dynamically changing images are extremely sentimental. The artistic re-creation of the translation retains the beauty of the original poem subtly. Using the connotations of Orient culture that the targeted readers have an intimate knowledge of in the Western culture makes translated poems produce resonance among them.

Take the verses of the poem *Returning to Mount Song* (《归嵩山作》) by Wang Wei as another example:

---

[1]   许渊冲.唐诗三百首新译 [M].北京：中国对外翻译出版公司，1988: 355.

清川带长薄，

车马去闲闲。

流水如有意，

暮禽相与还。

The limpid river, past its rushes,

Running slowly as my chariot.

Becomes a fellow voyager,

Returning home with the evening birds. (Tr. Witter Bynner)[①]

Witter Bynner blends the original four lines together into one sentence, which does not matter by itself but simplifies all the images. Obviously, his careless treatment cannot reflect the meaning the poem involves, not to mention the referential meaning of the images. Let's probe into the translation by Professor Xu Yuanchong, which is certainly more reasonable:

The limpid stream girdles a dense thicket,

Carriage pass on the way so leisurely.

Pairing birds fly home with me in the dusk,

And the flowing water seems quite friendly. (Tr. Xu Yuanchong)[②]

Another example is the second couplet from *A Spring View* (《春望》) by Du Fu. Look at the following two translations:

感时花溅泪，

恨别鸟惊心。

---

① BYNNER W, KIANG K H. The jade mountain: a Chinese anthology[M]. New York: Alfred A. Knopf, 1929:78.

② 许渊冲. 唐诗三百首新译 [M]. 北京：中国对外翻译出版公司, 1988: 195.

Where petals have been shed like tears

And lonely birds have sung their grief. (Tr. Witter Bynner)①

Blossoms invite my tears as in wild times they bloom;

The flitting birds stir my heart as I'm parted from home. (Tr. Xu Juntao)②

In these two lines the tear (泪) is the poet's tear and the heart (心) is also the poet's heart. Once again Bynner commits a mistake in the understanding of this semantic meaning owing to his finite knowledge of Chinese language and culture. Hence the first translation is full of confusion. Professor Wu gives a more acceptable translation in which the beautiful blossoms and flitting birds contrast sharply with the poet's anxiety about the revolt.

3.3   Aesthetic Equivalence of Cultural Image

The translation of cultural image is both a linguistic transference and an aesthetic representation, and is expected to obtain certain aesthetic equivalence. The preservation of the original poem's artistic charm is expected to be measured in the evaluation of a translated version, which is exactly in accordance with the principle of three-beauty put forward by Professor Xu Yuanchong: beauty in sense, sound and form. According to

---

① BYNNER W, KIANG K H. The jade mountain: a Chinese anthology[M]. New York: Alfred A.Knopf,1929:101.
② 许渊冲编.唐诗三百首新译 [Z]. 北京: 中国对外翻译出版公司 , 1988:151.

him, the aesthetic equivalence of the original cultural image is expected to be sought to the highest degree if possible, including all the three beauties. To obtain the beauty in sense, translators have to grasp the connotation or implication of the context. Besides, the devices like rhyme and rhythm employed in the original poetry to produce musicality are also expected to be preserved to achieve the beauty of sound. And the structural features such as the pattern, and line length of a poem should also be imitated to achieve the beauty in form.

3.3.1 Aesthetic Equivalence in Sense

The three-beauty principle is often credited as an inspiring but frankly polemical criterion, for it is feasible in theory but almost impossible in practice, at least difficult to achieve the beauty in all the three aspects. Therefore, Professor Xu specially points out that a poetic translation should be as beautiful as the original in sense, in sound and if possible in form. If the three beauties have conflict with each other, priority should be given to the beauty in sense, especially sense by cultural image.

Take two translations of two lines from Du Fu's *Thinking of My Brothers on a Moonlit Night*(《月夜忆舍弟》) for example:

露是今夜白，

月是故乡明。

The crystal dew is glittering at my feet,

The moon sheds, as of old, her silvery light. (Tr. H. A. Giles)[1]

---

[1] 詹晓娟. 李白诗歌英译历史 [M]. 成都：巴蜀书社，2017: 64

The season called the White Dew begins tonight,

Nowhere as in our native place is the moon so bright. (Tr. Wu Juntao)[①]

Obviously in the original "今夜" and "故乡" are the important background of the message expressed in the poem, which perfectly set off the poet's deep miss to his brothers and shape the main sense of the poem. Unfortunately, Mr. Giles does not render them into English and thus makes the translation eclipsed without aesthetic equivalence in sense. The second one retains these two expressions properly and does comparatively better in keeping the sensual beauty of the poem.

Another example is about the translation of "红颜" which frequently appears in Chinese literature. Take four lines from the poem *Ballad of a Merchant's Wife* (《长干行》) by Li Bai for example:

> 八月蝴蝶黄,
>
> 双飞西园草。
>
> 感此伤妾心,
>
> 坐愁红颜老。

In the eighth moon the butterflies pale their bright hues,

But in pairs they flit through the west glade,

With a pang I remember it, sitting alone,

Old in heart though my cheek does not fade. (Tr. C. Gaunt)[②]

September now!—the butterflies so gay

---

① 许渊冲 . 唐诗三百首新译 [M]. 北京 : 中国对外翻译出版公司 , 1988: 160.

② 吕叔湘 , 许渊冲 . 中诗英译比录 [M]. 香港 : 三联书店有限公司 , 1988:98.

Disport on grasses by our garden wall.

The sight my heart disturbs with longing woe.

I sit and wail, my red cheeks growing old. (Tr. W. J. B. Fletcher)①

And now, in the Eighth–month, yellowing butterflies

Hover, two by two, in our west–garden grasses.

And, because of all this, my heart is breaking.

And I fear for my bright cheeks, lest they fade. (Tr. Witter Bynner)②

It is the Eighth Month, the butterflies are yellow,

Two are flying among the plants in the west garden;

Seeing them, my heart is bitter with grief, they wound

the heart of the unworthy one.

The bloom of my face has faded, sitting with my sorrow. (Tr. Amy

Lowell)③

The yellow butterflies in autumn pass

Two by two o'er our western–garden grass.

This sight would break my heart, and I'm afraid,

Sitting alone, my rosy cheeks would fade. (Tr. Xu Yuanchong)④

① 吕叔湘,许渊冲.中诗英译比录 [M].香港:三联书店有限公司,1988:98.

② 吕叔湘,许渊冲.中诗英译比录 [M].香港:三联书店有限公司,1988:99.

③ 吕叔湘,许渊冲中诗英译比录 [M].香港:三联书店有限公司,1988: 100.

④ 吕叔湘,许渊冲中诗英译比录 [M].香港:三联书店有限公司,1988: 101.

The four lines describe the wife's worry and sorrow. The paired butterflies remind her of the past sweet time with her husband. Now, sitting alone, not only does she miss him, but she also worries that she is getting old. Chinese people like using "Hong Yan (红颜)" to symbolize that pretty young women rouge cheeks to keep their beauty. However, the first four translations of "Hong Yan" by foreigners respectively into "my face" "my red cheeks" "my bright cheeks" and "the bloom of my face" surely cannot let Western readers think of the beauty of a Chinese woman since in Western aesthetic appreciation the rosy cheeks are equal to a woman's beauty. So the translators fail to convey the essence of this image and therefore achieves no equivalence in sense. Fortunately, familiarity with the connotation of "Hong Yan" in Chinese enables Professor Xu to overcome the cultural barrier and maintain the symbolism of the image.

Let's probe into another example about " 西风 " in Huang Chao's *To the Chrysanthemum* (《 题菊花 》)

飒飒西风满院栽，蕊寒香冷蝶难来。

In soughing western wind you blossom far and nigh;

Your fragrance is too cold to invite butterfly. (Tr. Xu Yuanchong)[1]

"西风" in this poem is translated literally here because the image "western wind" in the original can be understood and accepted by target language readers easily with their common sense.

However, in some cases the sense of a image cannot be transferred

---

① 许渊冲 . 唐诗三百首新译 [M]. 北京 : 中国对外翻译出版公司 , 1988:356.

properly due to special linguistic or cultural barriers. One example is about the Chinese character "Liu（柳）", which refers to a willow twig/ tree on the surface, but associates itself with parting since it has a similar pronunciation to "Liu（留）", which means to stay, namely a homophony. It is a custom in the Tang Dynasty to break off a willow twig to see off a friend and "Liu（柳）" becomes a well-known imagery in Chinese culture. Look at the following lines quoted respectively from Wang Zhihuan's *Ci-poem of Liangzhou*（王之涣，688—742《凉州词》）and Wang Wei's *A Farewell Song*（《渭城曲》）：

羌笛何须怨杨柳，

春风不度玉门关。

O why *Qiang*'s flutes over willows sad will wail away?

The spring wind has never ventured west of Jade-Pass' way. (Tr. Xu Yuanchong)[1]

渭城朝雨浥轻尘，

客舍青青柳色新。

No dust is raised on pathways wet with morning rain,

The willows by the tavern look so fresh and green. (Tr. Xu Yuanchong)[2]

However, once the word "Liu（柳）" loses its original sound in another language, the cultural implication disappears, too. When rendering such an image, the translator has no choice but to give an annotation to clarify the implied meaning in order to help foreign readers gain some insights into the beauty in sense.

---

① 许渊冲．唐诗三百首新译 [M]．北京：中国对外翻译出版公司，1997:251.

② 许渊冲．唐诗三百首新译 [M]．北京：中国对外翻译出版公司，1988:117.

3.3.2   Aesthetic Equivalence in Sound

The sound in Chinese classical poetry is also an important part to show the cultural imagery of the original. Of course, tuneful rhyme and melodious rhythm of a translation are the key factors that determine the musical beauty of itself and the aesthetic equivalence in sound between the two texts. The use of rhyme is an essential component of the musical effect in sound and thus the typical feature of verse writing, including poetry. Take a look again at *Ci-poem on Liangzhou* by Wang Zhihuan as an example in point:

黄河远上白云间，

一片孤城万仞山。

羌笛何须怨杨柳，

春风不度玉门关。

The Yellow River rises remote in clouds all dim,

Alone a castle's perched 'mid soaring peaks so grim.

O why *Qiang'* flutes over "willows" sad will wail away?

The spring wind has never ventured west of Jade-Pass' way.

(Tr. Xu Yuanchong)[1]

In this poem, " 间 " (jian) in the first line, " 山 " (shan) in the second line and "关" (guan) in the last line rhyme with each other by the foot "an" . It can be noticed that in four-line poetry, a quatrain, there is always an unrhymed character in the third line which plays a part in producing a switch of a sound to avoid monotony. Thus the rhyme-scheme of this

---

[1]   许渊冲 . 唐诗三百首新译 [M]. 北京：中国对外翻译出版公司 , 1997:251.

poem can be briefly denoted as *aaba*, while the English version changes the rhyme-scheme into *aabb*. Therefore, this poem both in Chinese version and in English version sounds catchy and tuneful. While reading this poem aloud with emotions, readers can easily appreciate its musical artistry and metrical flavor, and the aesthetic equivalence in sound remains.

Chinese is a tonal language and each Chinese character is monosyllabic and is pronounced in a fixed tone. In Chinese, there are four tones: level, rising, entering and falling. The level tone is horizontal and steady, the rising tone loud and clear, the entering tone high and melodious, and the falling tone short and rapid. Different arrangement of these four tones in poetry can achieve a melodious auditory effect. For metrical purposes, the first two tones are considered to be even tones, i.e. *pingsheng* (平声), while the other two be oblique tones, i.e. *zesheng* (仄声). The change in arrangement of even and oblique tones within and between lines leads to the modulation in pitch and features in the auditory beauty of Chinese classical poetry. The versification rule requires that the patterned sequence of different tones of one line, especially the second, fourth and sixth characters, must contrast with that of the next line basically in terms of even tone (marked by "—") and oblique tone (marked by " | "). However, in the appreciation of English poetry, attention is paid to metre: division of a line into rhythmical units called feet by the regular recurrence of stressed syllables and unstressed ones, such as iambus and trochee. The first one is a stressed syllable (marked by "–") followed by an unstressed one (marked by "v") and the other is reversed. Take again *A Farewell Song* by Wang Wei as an example :

| — — | | — —

渭 城 朝 雨 浥 轻 尘,

| — — — | | —

客 舍 青 青 柳 色 新。

| — | | | — |

劝 君 更 尽 一 杯 酒,

— — — — — | —

西 出 阳 关 无 故 人。

v — v —   v —   v —   v   — v   —

No dust is raised on pathways wet with morning rain,

v — v v v — v   — v — v   —

The willows by the tavern look so fresh and green.

— v —   v v   — v — v   — v —

I invite you to drink a cup of wine again,

—   v v — v   — v   —   —   v v —

West of the Southern Pass no more friends will be seen.(Tr. Xu Yuanchong)[1]

The interlacing presentation of even and oblique tones in the original as well as the stressed and unstressed syllables in the translation produces the rising and falling tendency of word sounds, which echoes within and between the lines and forms a strong sense of rhythm. The sweet cadence can delight the ear and the heart of readers and bring them into the scene

---

① 许渊冲 . 唐诗三百首新译 [M]. 北京：中国对外翻译出版公司 , 1997:117.

described in the poem. Thus the rhythm naturally helps to unfold a picture of seeing-off and to express their sincere friendship and thus enhances the appreciation of the poem. Hence the beauty in sound is almost not lost and the aesthetic equivalence in sound stays.

Take the first four lines of *Drinking Alone with the Moon* (《月下独酌》) by Li Bai as another example：

花间一壶酒，

独酌无相亲。

举杯邀明月，

对影成三人。

A cup of wine, under the flowering trees；

I drink alone, for no friend is near.

Raising my cup I beckon the bright moon,

'For he, with my shadow, will make three men. (Tr. Arthur Waley)[1]

An arbor of flowers

And a kettle of wine：

Alas! In the bowers

No companion is mine.

Then the moon sheds her rays

On my goblet and me,

And my shadow betrays

---

[1] WALEY A. A hundred and seventy Chinese poems[M].London: Constable and Company Ltd., 1918: 118

We're a party of three. (Tr. Herbert A. Giles)[①]

In the original the vivid cultural images like "flowers" "wine" "moon" and "shadow" succeed to shape the mood of loneliness, and the poem is obviously beautiful in sound. Giles' translation changes the original four lines into eight with four antithetic rhymes /auə/, /aɪn/, /eɪz/, and /iː/ , and the rhythm is also catching and melodious, and therefore, the aesthetic equivalence is creatively reproduced. However, Waley creates "sprung rhythm" , setting five quantitative stressed syllables and non-stressed syllables in each line: a cup of wine, under the flowering trees/I drink alone, for no friend is near/Raising my cup I beckon the bright moon/For he, with my shadow, will make three men. In this way, the translated poems have a clear sense of rhythm, which not only retains the beauty of Chinese poetry in sound, but also has the sense of rhythm of English poetry, and is more natural and flexible than that of metrical poetry.

Sometimes, it is the special sound in wording that highlights the aesthetic beauty and harmony of the cultural image. J. Addison once characterized beauty as the harmonious adaptation of parts to the whole. Thus in translation it is through the agency of harmony that the translator is able to grasp the whole image, and it is by means of the holistic qualities of imagery mentally actualized that he is able to create an aesthetic equivalence with beauty.

Another typical example comes from Du Fu's *The Army Carts* (《兵车行》):

车辚辚，马萧萧，

---

① 吕叔湘，许渊冲．中诗英译比录 [M]．香港：三联书店有限公司，1988: 261.

行人弓箭各在腰。

Carts rumbling, horses neighing,

Men march with bows and arrows at their waists. (Tr. Yang Xianyi)[①]

The war-chariots rattle; the war-horses whinny.

Each man of you has a bow and a quiver at his belt. (Tr. Witter Bynner)[②]

Chariots rumble and roll; horses whinny and neigh.

Footmen at their girdle bows and arrows display. (Tr. W. J. B. Fletcher)[③]

In the original poem the repetition of sounds "Lin Lin (辚 辚)" and "Xiao Xiao (萧萧)", which are also two images, vividly depict the chaos and tensions before the war. Professor Yang only translates then simply into "rumbling" and "neighing" respectively with correct semantic equivalence but achieves no aesthetic equivalence in sound. In the second translation the word "war" is added twice, which can help form a kind of tension in both meaning and voice. In the third translation, Fletcher manages to render them by using two words together respectively. The combination of "rumble and roll" and "whinny and neigh" does better in expressing the pre-war atmosphere, especially when reading with stressed voice. In addition, the end of the two lines rhyme each other with vowel /eɪ/, which succeeds in achieving the equivalence in sound. As a result, the readers may be able to imagine

---

① 吕叔湘，许渊冲 . 中诗英译比录 [M] 香港：三联书店有限公司，1988:322.

② 吕叔湘，许渊冲 . 中诗英译比录 [M] 香港：三联书店有限公司，1988:322.

③ 吕叔湘，许渊冲 . 中诗英译比录 [M]. 香港：三联书店有限公司，1988: 323.

the dusk kicked up by the chariots and horses and can feel the tension and horror of the war around the corner.

3.3.3 Aesthetic Equivalence in Form

Beauty in form is mainly about the poetic pattern, the length of line and parallelism, etc. Under the premise of the successful conveyance of sense and sound in rendition, the form may be considered to be another significant part to make the whole translation more enjoyable. Parallelism is an important term in Chinese classical poetry and refers to antithesis between two lines matched in sound and sense, especially forming a contrast by using contradictory or similar ideas in sharp juxtaposition. It requires that in a antithesis couplet, basically the characters in each line are identical in number, and that words in the same places should be of the same part of speech. The words in parallelism had better respond to each other in ideas and tones: ideas being analogous or opposed while even tones matching oblique tones. This point may be perfectly illustrated by the first couplet in Li Bai's *Farewell to a Friend* (《送友人》):

青 山 横 北 郭,

| | | | |

白 水 绕 东 城。

Green mountains bar the northern sky;(Tr. Xu Yuanchong)[1]

| | | | | | |

White   water   girds the eastern town.

---

① 许渊冲 . 唐诗三百首新译 [M]. 北京：中国对外翻译出版公司，1997:133.

This couplet takes the grammatical pattern of *adj.* (green—white) + *n.* (mountains—water) + *v.* (bar—gird) + *adj.* (northern—eastern) + *n.* (sky—town). Both the Chinese and English version are in perfect parallelism by literal translation. Hence this translation retains a perfect aesthetic equivalence in form.

Take three translations of the poem *Passionate Grief*(《怨情》) by Li Bai as another example:

美人卷珠帘，

深坐颦蛾眉。

但见泪痕湿，

不知心恨谁。

Beautiful is this woman who rolls up the pearl—reed blind.

She lies in an inner chamber,

And her eyebrows, delicate as a moth's antennae,

Are drawn with grief.

One sees only the wet lines of tears.

For whom does she suffer this misery?

We do not know. (Tr. Amy Lowell)[①]

My lady has rolled up the curtains of pearl,

And sits with a frown on her eyebrows apart.

Wet traces of tears can be seen as they curl.

But who knows for whom is the grief in her heart? (Tr. W. J. B. Fletcher)[②]

---

① 吕叔湘，许渊冲.中诗英译比录 [M].香港：三联书店有限公司，1988:276.

② 吕叔湘，许渊冲.中诗英译比录 [M].香港：三联书店有限公司，1988:276.

A fair girl draws the blind aside,

And sadly sits with drooping head;

I see her burning tear-drops glide,

But know not why those tears are shed. (Tr. H. A. Giles)[①]

Obviously, the first translation is a rewritten version with seven lines which are too diverse in length and thus there is no beauty in form. The second and third translations remain four lines to keep the formal equivalence. Especially, the third one, by adding the invisible subject "I", is a compound sentence, constituting two completely independent clauses connected with a semi-colon, and makes the poem structurally antithetic. Hence the achievement of the aesthetic equivalence in form.

It has been discussed previously that poets often adopt well-balanced forms to organize the cultural imagery to display their special emotions. Whether or not the translators can copy or imitate the balanced structure in translation will to a great extent influence the beauty in form. Take two translations of the poem *Sitting Alone in Mt. Jingting* (《独坐敬亭山》) by Li Bai as an example:

众鸟高飞尽,

孤云独去闲。

相看两不厌,

只有敬亭山。

Multitudes of birds have all flown high up away.

---

① 吕叔湘,许渊冲.中诗英译比录[M].香港:三联书店有限公司,1988:277.

The solitary cloud is drifting alone idly farther and farther away.

Both Mount Jingting and I are looking at each other intently and untiredly,

The former being the sole one who keeps me company. (Tr. Tang Yihe)[①]

All birds have flown away, so high;

A lonely cloud drifts on, so free.

We are not tired, the Peak and I,

Nor I of him, nor he of me. (Tr. Xu Yuanchong)[②]

In the original, the cultural imagery in the first two lines depicts the poet's depression after being demoted and his pure love to the nature. "众鸟" and "孤云", "高" and "独", "飞" and "去", "尽" and "闲" are in strict balance in form, whose beauty also adds much to that of the sense of the poem. Comparatively, the first translation succeeds in rendering the basic meaning of the poem but fails to keep the antitheism in form. Clearly the second translation does better in achieving the aesthetic equivalence in form through the balanced wording of "birds" and "cloud", "flown away" and "drifts on", "so high" and "so free".

In summary, the image is rooted in culture and cultural image is the soul of classical poetry. Rich of deep connotations, cultural image can help to understand the poem on one hand but may enhance the difficulty of its translation on the other hand. Whether the cultural imagery is decoded correctly or not will have an influence on the receptors' appreciation of

---

① 唐一鹤.英译唐诗三百首 [M].天津:天津人民出版社,2005: 98.

② 许渊冲.唐诗三百首新译 [M].北京:中国对外翻译出版公司,1988: 63.

the original poem. The transference of cultural imagery serves as a key to the attempts of keeping the original grace and elegance and it is a dynamic process of continuous adapting and choosing. Semantic equivalence of cultural imagery is considered to be the basic requirement of cultural imagery translation and aesthetic equivalence of cultural imagery is claimed to be the ideal standard of cultural image translation, including equivalence in sense, sound and form.

Chapter 4   The Strategies of Cultural Image Translation

Susan Bassnett holds that though a poem cannot be transferred between two different languages, it can nevertheless be transplanted. People will place the seed in the new soil, and then a new plant will develop. To determine and locate that seed and to set about its transplantation is the task of the translator.[①] In the translation of Chinese classical poetry, it's a hard job to deliver the connotation that images have correctly. Considering the characteristics of the cultural image, a good translation should facilitate the target language readers to comprehend both denotation and connotation the cultural image possesses, allowing for a smooth exchange of information between different cultures as well as different languages. Therefore, translators are expected to cultivate intercultural awareness, just as Eugene Nida says, "It is always assumed that translators are at least bilingual, but this is not enough. To be a fully competent translator, one also needs to be bicultural in order to read between the lines" . [②] This also

---

① BASSNETT S. Translation studies[M]. Shanghai: Shanghai Foreign Language Education Press, 2004: 85.

② NIDA E A. Language, culture and translating[M]. Shanghai: Shanghai Foreign Language Education Press, 1993: 109.

requires translators to use their creative power to give the original text a new life. Professor Xu argues that a good translation with inspiration is like a reincarnation, which makes people feel a new recreation and that a mechanical translation is like a dead bird, which saves up the appearance and the body but cannot fly.

4.1　Preservation of the Original Image with Cultural Overlap

Cultural overlap means the situation in which imagery exists in both source culture and target culture and bears the same denotation and connotation, since in many aspects human experience and observation of the world are similar under the similar living surroundings. In this case, the cultural image can be preferably kept in rendering the form as well as the content so that the target readers can appreciate the beauty of the translation as equivalent as what the source readers receive from the original text. The ideal approach is literal translation to reproduce the original imagery. Newmark once pointed out: "in communicative as in semantic translation, provided that an equivalent effect is secured, the literal word-for-word translation is not only the best, but also the only valid method of translation" . [1]

In Chapter 2 it is argued that both in Chinese and English the moon can express loneliness since it hangs alone in the sky, so this image can be

---

[1]　NEWMARK P. Approaches to translation[M]. Shanghai: Shanghai Foreign Language Education Press, 2001: 39.

transferred directly in translation. Take *Longing on Marble Steps* (《玉阶怨》) by Li Bai for example：

玉阶生白露，

夜久侵罗袜。

却下水晶帘，

玲珑望秋月。

The marble steps with dew grow white,

It soaks her gauze socks late at night.

She lowers the crystal screen,

And gazes at the moon, pale and bright. (Tr. Wan Zhaofeng)[①]

On the surface, the poem simply depicts a picture of a woman gazing at the moon silently at night. But at the emotional level, it really expresses her deep missing and longing for her lover or husband. It's implied in the first two lines that it is a chilly late night, when the moon appears more lonely. The poet relies entirely on an integrated succession of images to suggest rather than state the reason for the lament, so her secret grievance has been concealed implicitly without a single explicit word. All the images including the moon are translated directly into English with no connotation lost and the theme also appears clearly beyond the words.

Take three translation versions of the first two lines in *Passionate Grief* (《怨情》) also by Li Bai as an example：

美人卷珠帘，

深坐颦蛾眉。

---

① 辜正坤. 译学津原 [M]. 郑州：文心出版社，2005: 96.

A fair girl draws the blind aside,

And sadly sits with drooping head. (Tr. H. A. Giles)[①]

A lovely woman rolls up the delicate bamboo blind.

She sits deep within twitching her moth eyebrows. (Tr. S. Obata)[②]

A lady fair uprolls the screen,

With eyebrows knit she waits in vain. (Tr. Xu Yuanchong)[③]

There are three cultural images in these two lines "Mei Ren (美 人)" "Zhu Lian (珠 帘)" and "E Mei (娥 眉)". The three literal renderings of "Mei Ren" are out of question. The second translation of "Zhu Lian" into "bamboo blind" reflects the translator's subjective assertion since a blind is not always made of bamboo, from which "Zhu (珠)" is very much far. In addition, "E Mei" is equivalent to eyebrows in English culture, so the first rendition that changes it into "drooping head" is unnecessary.

Take Wang Wei's poem *Deer Park* (《鹿柴》) as another instance:

空山不见人，

但闻人语响。

返景入深林，

复照青苔上。

Empty valley—no man in sight.

<hr>

① 吕叔湘，许渊冲.中诗英译比录 [M].香港：三联书店有限公司，1988：323.

② 吕叔湘，许渊冲.中诗英译比录 [M].香港：三联书店有限公司，1988：324.

③ 吕叔湘，许渊冲.中诗英译比录 [M].香港：三联书店有限公司，1988：325.

But some voices echo, far and light.

Deep woods—the light of the parting day

Returns, lingering upon the green moss. (Tr. Zhu Chushen)[①]

In the original poem the static images "空山""返景""青苔" and the dynamic image "人语" have no special associative meanings and are retained in the translation. But they together constitute a clear contrast between sound and silence. It's in this way that the tranquility of the valley and the leisure of the poet are not broken but strengthened. The preservation of the images directly achieves equivalent effect that readers of both original and translated version can get insight into the theme of the poem.

Take four lines from *Song of the Northern Frontier* (《燕歌行》) by Gao Shi as the example:

> 战士军前半死生,
>
> 美人帐下犹歌舞。
>
> 大漠穷秋塞草腓,
>
> 孤城落日斗兵稀。

Half of our warriors lie killed on the battleground

While pretty girls in the camp sing and dance round.

Grass withers in the desert as autumn is late,

At sunset few men guard the lonely city gate. (Tr. Xu Yuanchong)[②]

The first two lines describe the sharply different living states between the warriors and the generals: the former have to shed blood and even fight

---

①　辜正坤.译学津原 [M].郑州:文心出版社,2005: 35.

②　许渊冲.唐诗三百首新译 [M].北京:中国对外翻译出版公司,1988: 98.

to death while the latter are indulged in sensual pleasure. The warriors are so brave, but they still lose the war just because of the incompetence and fatuity of the generals up to higher leaders. The last two lines help to depict the harshness and cruelty of the war. As a whole, the image of war is conducive to voicing the poet's wishes for a life of peace, stability and prosperity. These concrete images are translated directly into English with no loss of detonation and connotation and equivalence in both semantic and aesthetic levels are achieved successfully.

Look at Wang Wei's *The Warble Ravine*（《鸟鸣涧》）:

> 人闲桂花落，夜静春山空。
>
> 月出惊山鸟，时鸣春涧中。

Man at leisure, laurel flower fall.

Night silent, spring mountain empty.

Moon rise, startle mountain bird,

Time and time sing amidst spring brook. (Tr. A. C. Graham)[1]

The three words "man" "moon" and "night" in the poem do not have any modifying elements. They tend to refer to time and place rather than specific things. Therefore, the poem seems to be made up of "man" "bird" "moon" and "mountain", which constitute a simple and natural world. It's literal translation that makes the image reproduce in the translation. Once it's translated in standard English, the original meaning is destroyed.

Walking at leisure we watch Laurel flowers falling.

---

[1]　吕叔湘，许渊冲. 中诗英译比录 [M]. 香港：三联书店有限公司，1988: 325.

In the silence of this night the spring mountain is empty.

The moon rises, the birds are startled.

As they sing occasionally near the spring fountain. (Tr. Bai Ying)[1]

That "man" has become "us", which indicates all people enjoying the spring scenery have been included; "night" has become an individual "this night"; "bird" has become many birds after adding the plural suffix "s". The original meaning of the translation can only be maintained if the tenses, article and plural changes are deleted completely.

4.2   Adaptation of the Original Image with Cultural Parallelism

Cultural parallelism refers to the situation in which both source culture and target culture enjoy the same connotation with different denotations, expressed by different images. Therefore, when the substitution in the target language can be found to replace the counterpart in the source culture with equivalent effect, adaptation of the original image is preferred in the priority of target readers' comprehension, though the underlying functions of that may be missing in the target text to some degree. Take three translation versions of the two lines from the poem *A Beauty* (《佳人》) by Du Fu for example:

夫婿轻薄儿，

新人美如玉。

---

① 辜正坤 . 译学津原 [M]. 郑州 : 文心出版社 ,2005:142.

My husband is a frivolous guy;

Beautiful as jade, he's got a new bride. (Tr. Tang Yihe)[①]

My husband is a light-hearted bonny,

He then married another fair lady. (Tr. Wu Juntao)[②]

My husband is flirtatious enough,

to marry another girl sweet as a lily. (Tr. John Turner)[③]

Literally, "Mei Ru Yu (美如玉)" means "pretty as jade" since the image "Yu (玉)" always symbolizes beauty and luck in Chinese culture. However, "jade" in English culture connotes a worn-out taste and also a vulgar woman. Hence the first rendition confuses the semantic meaning of the imagery, and the omission of the imagery in the second rendition loses the equivalent beauty in sense. In the third translation, the translator changes the imagery into "sweet as a lily", which is quite appropriate since the lily more naturally symbolizes beauty and innocence in English.

Take the last two lines of poem *To Master Pei, a Palace Official* (《赠阙下裴舍人》) by Qian Qi as an example:

献赋十年犹未遇，

羞将白发对华簪。

For years, alas, I've sent my writings to court all in vain,

① 唐一鹤.英译唐诗三百首 [M].天津：天津人民出版社，2005: 98.
② 许渊冲.唐诗三百首新译 [M].北京：中国对外翻译出版公司，1988: 206.
③ 辜正坤.译学津原 [M].郑州：文心出版社，2005:156.

And white-haired now, I'm mortified your regalia to see. (Tr. Wang Shiren)①

The poet's frustration after having taken part in the imperial examinations for many years without success is intensified. Now he has already been white-haired, so he feels a bit shameful facing the imperial examiners. In ancient China, "Hua Zan (华簪)" is a coronal decoration of the officials and here it is a cultural image referring to the examiner. The translator does not render it literally but employs the English image of regalia, which symbolizes royalty and indicates a high social status in English culture. Thus the readers in target culture can achieve an equivalent effect as the readers in the source culture.

Take two translations of the four lines from the poem *Lovesickness* (《长相思》) by Li Bai as another example:

天长地远魂飞苦，

梦魂不到关山难。

长相思，

摧心肝！

Hard for the soul to fly,

Over skies so long and earth so wide!

So high the passes, deep the tide,

The vision comes not to my side,

Yet mutual longings us enwrap,

---

① 辜正坤 . 译学津原 [M]. 郑州 : 文心出版社 , 2005: 123.

Until my very heartstrings snap. (Tr. W. J. B. Fletcher)[①]

My soul cannot fly over sky so vast nor earth so wide;

In dreams I cannot go through mountain pass to her side.

We are so far apart,

The yearning breaks my heart. (Tr. Xu Yuanchong)[②]

In this poem, the dynamic cultural image "Cui Xin Gan (摧 心 肝)" in Chinese is "hurt heart and liver" to connote deep sorrow. However, this connotation is expressed only by "breaking heart /heartstring", so the two translation versions mentioned above with small alteration in the image are more reasonable than word-for-word translation.

4.3　Amplification of the Original Image with Cultural Deficiency

Cultural deficiency means that the connotation of a cultural image in the source language does not find its trace in the target language and almost cannot be substituted by other proper images in the target language, or that any substitution may cause too much misunderstanding of the original text. Under such a circumstance, the translators had better amplify directly and creatively the connotation of the original imagery to make compensation for the cultural deficiency for the sake of the equivalent effect.

---

① 吕叔湘，许渊冲 . 中诗英译比录 [M]. 香港：三联书店有限公司，1988: 335.
② 吕叔湘，许渊冲 . 中诗英译比录 [M]. 香港：三联书店有限公司，1988: 336.

Take another two lines from the poem *Song of the Northern Frontier* (《燕歌行》) by Gao Shi for example:

铁衣远戍辛勤久，

玉箸应啼别离后。

Still at the front, iron armor is worn and battered thin.

And here at home food—sticks are made of jade tears. (Tr. Witter Bynner)[①]

In coats of mail they have served

so long on the frontiers,

Since they left home their wives shed

streams of impearled tears. (Tr. Xu Yuanchong)[②]

The first translation may cause some confusion to English readers for what "jade tears" are. In fact the image "玉箸" in Chinese culture originally means chopsticks made of jade, common in ancient China but often used metaphorically as tears. The tears can be modified by "impearled" to stress the sorrow and depression but cannot by "jade" which will make nonsense.

Take three translation versions of another four lines from Li Bai's *Ballad of a Merchant's Wife* (《长干行》) as an example:

郎骑竹马来，

绕床弄青梅。

同居长干里，

两小无嫌猜。

---

① 吕叔湘，许渊冲 . 中诗英译比录 [M]. 香港：三联书店有限公司，1988: 445.
② 吕叔湘，许渊冲 . 中诗英译比录 [M]. 香港：三联书店有限公司，1988: 446.

You riding came on hobby−horse astride,

And wreathed my bed with greengage branches.

At Chang−kan village long together dwelt

We children twain, and knew no petty strife. (Tr. W. J. B. Fletcher)[1]

You would come, riding on your bamboo horse,

And loiter about the bench with green plums for toys.

So we both dwelt in Chang−kan town,

We were two children, suspecting nothing. (Tr. S. Obata)[2]

You came by on bamboo stilts, playing horse,

 You walked about my seat, playing with blue plums.

And we went on living in the village of Chokan,

 Two small people, without dislike or suspicion. (Tr. Ezra Pound)[3]

On a hobby−horse he came upon the scene;

Around the well we played with plums still green.

We lived close neighbors on riverside lane,

Carefree and innocent, we children twain. (Tr. Xu Yuanchong)[4]

In the poem the cultural images "Zhu Ma (竹马 : hobby−horse)" and "Qing

---

① 吕叔湘, 许渊冲 . 中诗英译比录 [M]. 香港 : 三联书店有限公司 , 1988: 435.
② 吕叔湘, 许渊冲 . 中诗英译比录 [M]. 香港 : 三联书店有限公司 , 1988: 436.
③ 吕叔湘, 许渊冲 . 中诗英译比录 [M]. 香港 : 三联书店有限公司 , 1988: 437.
④ 吕叔湘, 许渊冲 . 中诗英译比录 [M]. 香港 : 三联书店有限公司 , 1988: 438.

Mei (青梅: greengage/green plum)" exist in both Chinese and English languages. Therefore, the literal translation is acceptable while "bamboo horse" in the second translation is a mistaken word-for-word rendition. Comparatively the dynamic image "Rao Chuang (绕床)" is ambiguous in understanding. The first two translations are acceptable to some extent since "Chuang (床)" can literally be a bed or a bench. However, *Ci Hai* (《辞海》) gives it another explanation as "the raised platform around a well", because in ancient China, a well is usually located at public places such as playground or winnowing-lot (扬场/稻床), which exists in the countryside today, with kids playing around and some fruit trees such as plum standing around there. Thus the fourth translation by Professor Xu is more reasonable to depict the picture of the cultural image, achieving the semantic equivalence.

Let's examine the last two lines of Huang Chao's *To the Chrysanthemum* (《题菊花》):

他年我若为青帝，

报与桃花一处开。

Some day if as Lord of Spring come into power,

I'd order you to bloom together with peach flower. (Tr. Xu Yuanchong)[①]

"青帝", as the image of the poem, is the Lord of Spring who gains the upper hand of the arrival of spring in the Chinese culture. It's also called as Dong Jun, who lives in the East. Xu Yuanchong does not adopt literal translation, but amplification, "Lord of Spring", imparting its cultural

---

① 许渊冲. 唐诗三百首新译 [M]. 北京：中国对外翻译出版公司，1988: 334.

connotation to the English readers. In the Greek mythology, there is another Goddess, Horae, who rules four seasons of the world. Xuyuanxchong's translation creates the cultural resonance among the targeted readers.

4.4   Omission of the Original Image with Cultural Insignificance

In Chinese classical poetry sometimes the image is carried by the use of proper names of people, places, and events unique in Chinese history. If the denotation or connotation of it is essential to the comprehension and appreciation of the whole poem, the equivalent effect should be retained. If the transference of the proper name to the translation is of insignificance and even bring about much confusion to the target readers, the image itself has to be omitted directly or sometimes by adding a footnote to give an annotation.

Take the poem *Later Road of Shu* (《蜀道后期》) by Zhang Shuo (张说, 667—730) for example:

客心争日月，

来往预期程。

秋风不相待。

先到洛阳城。

My eagerness chases the sun and the moon.

I number the days until I reach home.

The winds of autumn they wait not for me,

But hurry on thither where I would be. (Tr. W. J. B. Fletcher)①

Supposing that "Luoyang (洛阳)" is literally transferred to the target language, the foreign readers may most probably doubt whether there is any difference between "Luoyang" and other places and why the winds of autumn should hurry to there rather than other places. Here Fletcher omits the original image of place so as to remove potential misunderstanding or confusion but without any loss of semantic equivalence or aesthetic equivalence in sense.

Take again four translation versions of the two lines from Li Bai's famous poem *Ballad of a Merchant's Wife* (《长干行》) as an example:

常存抱柱信，

岂上望夫台。

You always kept the faith of Wei-sheng,

Who waited under the bridge, unafraid of death,

I never knew I was to climb the Hill of Wang-fu,

And watch for you these many days. (Tr. S. Obata)②

My troth to thee till death I keep for aye.

My eyes still gaze adoring on my lord. (Tr. W. J. B. Fletcher)③

For ever and for ever and for ever,

---

① 吕叔湘，许渊冲．中诗英译比录 [M]．香港：三联书店有限公司，1988：426.

② 吕叔湘，许渊冲．中诗英译比录 [M]．香港：三联书店有限公司，1988：427.

③ 吕叔湘，许渊冲．中诗英译比录 [M]．香港：三联书店有限公司，1988：428.

Why should I climb the look-out? (Tr. Ezra Pound)[1]

If you have the faith of Wei-sheng,

Why do I have to climb up the waiting tower?

Rather than break faith, you declared you'd die.

Who knew I'd live alone in a tower high? (Tr. Xu Yuanchong)[2]

The images "Bao Zhu Xin (抱柱信)" and "Wang Fu Tai (望夫台)" come from an allusion in Chinese history, saying that a passionate and loyal young man, Wei Sheng, tries his best to keep the promise of waiting for his deeply loved girl on a heavily raining night but is unfortunately swallowed by rolling water when clasping a bridge post. So in Chinese culture this imagery connotes a kind of firm faith and loyal love. They are quite obscure to Chinese readers, let alone Western readers. The first translation tries to literally keep the original images and exotic features of the poem, but the Western readers find it difficult to understand "the faith of Wei-sheng" without explanation. In fact, this allusion is quite complicated and impossibly transferred within a poetic structure unless a footnote is provided for reference. So the other translations omit the cultural imagery but rewrite the whole lines with the main connotation in attempt to achieve the closest natural equivalence.

Let's see an example from Liu Yuxi's *Memories at Jinling* (《金陵怀古》):

兴废由人事，山川空地形。

后庭花一曲，幽怨不堪听。

---

[1]　吕叔湘，许渊冲 . 中诗英译比录 [M]. 香港：三联书店有限公司，1988：429.
[2]　吕叔湘，许渊冲 . 中诗英译比录 [M]. 香港：三联书店有限公司，1988：430.

Man decides a state's rise and fall,

Hills and streams can do nothing at all.

O hear the captive ruler's song!

How can you bear his grief for long? (Tr. Xu Yuanchong)[①]

The image "后庭花" has a special historical meaning, which comes from a song composed by the Emperor Chen Shubao in Nan Dynasty. Descendants generally employ this phrase to signify Chen's extravagance and dissipation which brought about the collapse of Nan Dynasty.

Xu yuanchong translates it into "the captive ruler's song". In this way, the image is avoided but its connotation is expressed directly, which leads to a puzzle for readers who don't know this story. In case we just translate it as pin yin "hou ting hua" with an annotation to make the cultural background known, the targeted readers must understand the poet's meaning much better, and at the same time, this method retains the original image.

The above strategies are just the general approaches to appropriately manipulate the cultural image in classical poetry during Tang Dynasty. It is acknowledgeable that they cannot cover all the successful translation of the cultural image due to its complexity. However, the translator's task is to insist the principle that the constant core, the essential denotation and connotation, of the image in the original poem should be retained in the translation process. In other words, the equivalence at both semantic and

---

① 许渊冲 . 唐诗三百首新译 [M]. 北京 : 中国对外翻译出版公司 , 1988: 212.

aesthetic levels of the cultural image is expected to be kept to the largest

degree as the translator can in order that the closest natural equivalence

brings about the equivalent effect in the translation.

Chapter 5　Case Study on Cultural Image Translation

Due to the different backgrounds of China and Western countries, there must be a lot of differences in the cultural understanding of the same object, which are the causes of translation divergence. Chinese classical poetry has the characteristics of implicit in connotation, harmonious in metre, bright in rhythm and well-balanced in pattern. So far, no single theories or schools have given them a satisfactory understanding framework yet. Chinese classical poetry is a relatively independent language world, and its transference emphasizes the transmission of cultural connotation and aesthetic effect, which is supposed to be the transmission of language-image-meaning. That is, the image is the carrier of meaning, therefore, reflecting through the image and expressing through the image. However, English has an obvious character of expressing through language. Hence, the most significant features to differentiate English and Chinese is hypotaxis and parataxis. The following part will give us a comparison among some influential translators' works. After the detailed analysis, we will have a clear view about their methods of image translation.

5.1　Case Study of Herbert Allen Giles

Herbert Allen Giles (1845–1935) was a well-known British sinologist. His 26 years of life in China made him well understand Chinese people and its culture. All his life, he worked on the study of sinology and the spread of Chinese culture. The number of his works of sinology and translations were more than 60 involving many fields, including better versions of Chinese poetry he produced. About his translation Lytton Strachey said in *Characters and Commentaries*: "The book...is worth reading, not only for its curiosity, but for its beauty and charm..." "...it is through its mastery of the tones and depths of affection that our anthology hold a unique place in the literature of the world" . [1]And Arthur Waley praised Giles for uniting "rhyme and literalness with wonderful dexterity" . He sticked to Victorian metrical form in translating Chinese classical poetry. Because British classical poetics was dominated from the end of 19th century to the starting of the 20th century. The combination of light and heavy syllables and the consistence of feet and rhyme are not only the basic norms of the traditional British poetry art, but also the form of poetics which is generally recognized and accepted by the British readers at that period. Under that particular historical context, there is no doubt that British missionaries and diplomats translated and introduced Chinese poetry by following the rules of mainstream poetics. A

---

① 吕叔湘，许渊冲．中诗英译比录 [M]．香港：三联书店有限公司，1988: 115.

study on Giles' image translation of Tang poetry would shed light on the goal of this research. Take a look at Giles' *Ichabod* (《滕王阁诗》):

滕王高阁临江渚，佩玉鸣鸾罢歌舞。

画栋朝飞南浦云，珠帘暮卷西山雨。

闲云潭影日悠悠，物转星移几度秋。

阁中帝子今何在？槛外长江空自流。

Near these islands a palace was built by a prince,

But its music and song have departed long since;

The hill—mists of morning sweep down on the halls,

At night the red curtains lie furled on the walls.

The clouds o'er the water their shadow still cast,

Things change like the stars: how few autumns have passed,

And yet where is that prince? Where is he?—No reply,

Save the splash of the stream rolling ceaselessly by. (Tr. Herbert A. Giles)[1]

Influenced by the Six Dynasties' poetry, the altitude and long visits of the pavilion are famed for their parallelism. But from Giles' version, the targeted readers can't know the Pavilion is high and affords a magnificent view. The poet, Wang Bo, tells us the nature is never changing while the imperial country is. Here again Giles is wrong to say "how few autumns have passed". The poem's foothold is Pavilion, which is also the image of the poem. In the Western culture, building includes all the building of the

---

① 许渊冲. 中诗英韵探胜 [M] 北京：北京大学出版社，2010:139.

City. For instance, in Wordsworth's sonnet *Composed Upon Westminster Bridge,* "The city now doth like a garment wear...Ships, towers, domes, theatres and temples..." (Lv Shuxiang & Xu Yuanchong, 1988) However, what Chinese only focuses on is the colored beams and furled drapes/curtains in the pavilion, which fully reflects the Chinese language is indirect and suggestive. Giles mistakenly understands it, and of course, he imparts it to the targeted readers wrongly.

Another designed example can be taken as the one to explore the language differences and image differences between Chinese and English:

登幽州台歌

前不见古人，后不见来者。

念天地之悠悠，独怆然而涕下。

Regrets

My eyes saw not the men of old;

And now their age away had rolled.

I weep—to think I shall not see,

The heroes of posterity. (Tr. Herbert A. Giles)[①]

This poem is written during the poet's degradation on the watchtower of You Zhou which was built around 300 B.C. by the King of Yan. Now the degraded poet ascends the tower lonely. Naturally, the King Yan's success is linked with his frustration. The vastness of the earth contrasts against his solitude strongly. As for the image of loneliness, Giles' version makes

---

① 吕叔湘，许渊冲．中诗英译比录 [M]．香港：三联书店有限公司，1988: 132.

English readers feel deep regrets. However, it doesn't arouse the sympathy for the poet among the readers. In *Deserted Places* by Robert Frost: "In a field I looked into going past…The loneness includes me unawares, and lonely as it is, that loneliness… " [1]By comparing these two poems, the Chinese people feel lonely because of few people; the Western people feel lonely due to the fact he/ she is in the deserted places.

The moon is what we see in our daily life, but the poet injects his own eagerness into it, so it becomes lyrical and poetic. The following poem by Zhang Jiuling fully demonstrates it like this:

赋得自君之出矣

自君之出矣，不复理残机。

思君如满月，夜夜减清辉。

An Absent Husband

Since my lord left—ah me, unhappy hour!——

The half-spun web hangs idly in my bower;

My heart is like the full moon, full of pains,

Save that't is always full and never wanes. (Tr. Herbert A. Giles)[2]

In this poem, Zhang Jiuling describes a sorrowful picture that a wife misses her husband who is far from home by the means of comparing her heart to the full moon which wanes day by day. The poet also infuses the wife's sorrow and missing into the aggrieved moon in a tactful way. Successively, it also exacerbates the wife's sorrow. Giles' version succeeds

---

① 吕叔湘，许渊冲 . 中诗英译比录 [M]. 香港：三联书店有限公司，1988: 157.
② 吕叔湘，许渊冲 . 中诗英译比录 [M]. 香港：三联书店有限公司，1988: 429.

in imparting the wife's missing heart to the painful moon. In this context, the readers can fully understand the reason why the wife is so immersed in woe that she cannot go on weaving.

In Shelley's *To Mary*:

...I am not well whilst thou art far;

As sunset to the sphered moon,

As twilight to the western star.

Thou, beloved, art to me.

O Mary dear, that you were here;

The Castle echo whispers 'Here!'

We can sense the deep missing for his wife from Shelley's poem. Whether it's the full moon in China or the sphered moon in the West, the poet always utilizes the image of the moon to accentuate the love for her husband/ his wife.

When it comes to Giles' translation of Chinese poetry, we often mention the rules and forms of traditional English poetry he strictly sticks to. For example, He Zhizhang's *The Return*:

少小离家老大回，乡音无改鬓毛衰。

儿童相见不相识，笑问客从何处来。

Bowed down with age I seek my native place,

Unchanged my speech, my hair is silvered now;

My very children do not know my face,

But smiling ask, "O, stranger, whence art thou?" (Tr. Herbert A. Giles)①

The background in which this poem is created is that the poet returns back to his native land at the age of 84. In Line 1–2 is a forceful contrast in the time span, his unchanged accent at his young age and his changed hair at his old age. In Line 3–4 his sorrow is expressed not in a sad scene but in a merry tone, not by what he says but by what the children ask. The readers can feel the poet's emotion touched off by the children's curiosity and recollected in tranquility. Giles' translation "my very children" indicates that the children he met might be his grandsons or granddaughters or children of other villagers, making it more lyrical than the original poem for the old poet not to be recognized by his own grandchildren. This quatrain follows the iambic tetrameter: the first two lines *ab*; the last two lines still *ab*. It is loyal to the original poem from the layer of the meaning, and it is a successful poem translated by Giles who always insists on the rhyme but destroys the meaning and widely received by English readers.

The theme of the life and death reflected in the poem is always constant in English. For example, in Wordsworth's *We Are Seven*, the English maid does not recognize her brother John and her sister Jane as dead, ②while the Chinese poet does not recognize his grandchildren. To some extent, the theme of life and death is eternal at all times and in all countries.

---

① 许渊冲 . 中诗英韵探胜 [M] 北京: 北京大学出版社 ,2010:141.
② 吕叔湘 , 许渊冲 . 中诗英译比录 [M] 香港 : 三联书店有限公司 , 1988: 376.

5.2　Case Study of Arthur Waley

In the early 20th century, British sinologist Arthur Waley (1888–1966) made a great contribution in the translation of Chinese poetry in the ancient times. His translation work is simple and direct, without so many profound meanings, which is deemed to be the attraction of Chinese classical poetry. His famous work *One Hundred and Seventy Chinese Poems* has become a classic and authoritative work for Western sinologists to translate Chinese ancient poetry. After that, it has been reproduced many times, and its influence has surpassed the British academic circle. The book is composed of two parts: Walley's articles and his poetry translation. The content of the paper is about Waley's untangling of ancient Chinese poetry and his translation theory, for example, *The Limitations of Chinese Literature*, *The Rise and Progress of Chinese Poetry* and *The Method of Translation*. Later, Waley produces *More Translations From the Chinese*.

Concerning the image in Tang poetry, influenced by Ezra Pound and imagists, he attaches great importance to the image of poetry and regards it as the soul of poetry. "I adopt literal translation...I try to avoid adding my own image in my translation, and at the same time, I don't delete the image inherent in the original poem." [1] "When translating Chinese poetry, I try to make my translation close to the original poem, and I just want to make a

---

[1]　WALEY A. A hundred and seventy Chinese poems[M].London: Constable and Company Ltd.,1918: 44.

little manipulation," Waley said in an interview with Roy Fuller. It can be seen that Waley's translation is as faithful to the original as possible. The following is the treatment of images in his English translation of Bai Juyi's poem:

夜泊旅望

少睡多愁客，中宵起望乡。

沙明连浦月，帆白满船霜。

近海江弥阔，迎秋夜更长。

烟波三十宿，犹未到钱唐。

On the Way to Hangchow: Anchor on the River at Night

Little sleeping and much grieving,—the traveler

Rises at midnight and looks back towards home.

The sands are bright with moonlight that joins the shores;

The sail is white with dew that has covered the boat.

Nearing the sea, the river grows broader and broader:

Approaching autumn, the nights longer and longer.

Thirty times we have not reached Hangchow. (Tr. Arthur Waley)[①]

This poem is written in the second year of Changqing (822) when Bai Juyi arrived in Hangzhou from Chang'an in the journey. Bai Juyi's feelings of homesickness and sorrow in his journey is transmitted. Among them, there is poet's worry about his future and the hardships of the world. The images are mainly concentrated on bright moonlight, like the sandy bank, waterfront, sails, open and wide river, all these forming the

---

① Arthur Waley. A Hundred and Seventy Chinese Poems[Z].New York: Alfred A. Knopf,1918:165.

scene of the autumn night. The series of images create an empty and cold poetic conception. Images in the original poem have not been increased or deleted in Waley's translation. The reflection of the inner logic and artistic conception that the original poem contains can be said to be a masterpiece in literal translation.

In order to illustrate that Waley focuses on the faithfulness to the original, a comparative analysis of Waley's poems and those of other translators can show that he lays stress on images. Have a look at Waley's and Xu Yuanchong's translation on Li Bai's poem *Going Down Chung-Nan Mountain and Spending the Night Drinking with the Hermit Tou-Ssu*(《下终南山过斛斯山人宿置酒》) respectively:

> 暮从碧山下，山月随人归。
>
> 却顾所来径，苍苍横翠微。
>
> 相携及田家，童稚开荆扉。
>
> 绿竹入幽径，青萝拂行衣。
>
> 欢言得所憩，美酒聊共挥。
>
> 长歌吟松风，曲尽河星稀。
>
> 我醉君复乐，陶然共忘机。

At dusk we left the blue mountain-head;

The mountain-moon followed our homeward steps.

We looked round: the path by which we had come

Was a dark cleft across the shoulder of the hill.

Hand in hand we reached the walls of the farm;

A young boy opened the wicker-gate.

Through green bamboos a deep road ran

Where dark creepers brushed our coats as we passed.

We were glad at last to come to a place of rest,

With wine enough to drink together to our fill,

Long I sang to the tune of the Pine-tree wind;

When the song was over, the river-stars were few.

I was drunk and you happy at my side;

Till mingled joy drove the world from our hearts. (Tr. Arthur Waley) ①

At dusk I leave the hills behind,

The moon escorts me all the way.

Looking back, I see the path wind,

Across the woods so green and grey.

We come to your cot hand in hand,

Your lad opens the gate for me.

Bamboos along the alley stand,

And vines caress my cloak with glee.

I'm glad to talk and drink good wine,

Together with my hermit friend.

We sing the songs of wind and pine,

And stars are set when singings end.

I'm drunk and you're merry and glad:

① WALEY A. A hundred and seventy Chinese poems[M].London: Constable and Company Ltd., 1918: 172.

We both forget the world is sad. (Tr. Xu Yuanchong)[1]

This poem is written by Li Bai when he was worshiping the Imperial Academy in the capital of Tang Dynasty, Chang'an. He describes the scenery that the poet sees on the way down the mountain on the moonlit night of Zhongnan mountain, and visits a hermit to stay at his home. They sit face to face, talking and drinking. The poem combines narration, scenery-describing with lyricism, showing the beauty of natural scenery, and Li Bai's natural and unrestrained talent and the resonance with his friends in his spiritual pursuit. The poem's purpose lies in the last line "till mingled joy drove the world from our hearts".

The images of the whole poem play a significant role in the narration and the foil of emotion. As far as the image translation of the two translated poems is concerned, it seems that Waley's translation is more loyal to the original. The following table is the translation of the six images of "碧山" "山月" "荆扉" "绿竹" "青萝" and "河星" by Waley and Xu Yuanchong, which can reflect the difference between the two versions.

	碧山	山月	荆扉	绿竹	青萝	河星
Waley	blue mountain-head	mountain-moon	wicker-gate	green bamboos	dark creepers	river-stars
Xu Yuanchong	hills	moon	gate	bamboos	vines	stars

In addition to the translation of "青萝", all the other images present

---

① 许渊冲 . 唐诗三百首新译 [M]. 北京：中国对外翻译出版公司，1988: 322.

the atmosphere created by the images of the original poem. However, Xu Yuanchong's translation has reduced the attributes to modify the images appearing in the original poem for conciseness such as hills, moon, gate, bamboos, vines and stars. As for the translation of "翠微", Xu Yuanchong stresses its color, and the woods are so green and grey; Waley translates it into "the shoulder of the hill". From the whole, "苍苍" means boundless mountain air, while "翠微" also means the mountain mists. Hence, it is proper to translate it into "the shoulder of the hill". Waley's image translation is faithful to the original poem to a great extent, although sometimes it is inevitable to make mistakes.

Let's probe into Waley's *On Seeing the Ruins of the King of Yueh's Palace* (《越中览古》).

越王勾践破吴归，义士还乡尽锦衣。

宫女如花满春殿，只今惟有鹧鸪飞。

The King of Yueh shattered Wu and came home again;

His soldiers dispersed to their villages and donned embroidered clothes.

His court ladies like flowers filled the Spring Palace,

Now what is left? What but the wild swan's flight? (Tr. Arthur Waley)[1]

This poem is about Li Bai's feeling about the battle between Wu and Yue in 770-476 B.C. This poem is written based on the historical events of hegemonism. It expresses the past victories with the materials of Goujian's final extermination of Wu and the return of the royal guards to their

---

① WALEY A. A hundred and seventy Chinese poems[M].London: Constable and Company Ltd., 1918: 172.

hometown. Fame, glory and wealth are just a drop in the bucket. Being part of the historical symbolic images, the allusion of this poem lies in the first sentence "The King of Yueh shattered Wu and came home again". When it comes to Goujian in the Chinese culture, we think of his "enduring the hardships by sleeping on the brushwood and tasting the gall". However, Waley does not make any note about it. The two pictures of prosperity and decline in Yueh's Palace, forming the contrast, embodies the rule of ups and downs in the world.

Waley holds the banner of literal translation, creatively sets off the pattern of Tang poetry with "sprung rhythm" which makes the original work continue its life and assure its survival, emphasizes image translation in Tang poetry translation, chooses less poems with more allusions, and deals with the special grammar of Tang poetry based on the restoration of the original poetry style. His translated poems generally show the characteristics of the source language culture, which makes an important contribution to building the bridge of cultural exchange between China and West.

5.3　Case Study of Weng Xianliang

Weng Xianliang is a famed translator, who died at his young age, so he didn't have many translated works on ancient poetry and the documents of translation research. However, it's his *An English Translation of Chinese Ancient Poems* (《古诗英译》) alone that is enough to establish his representative position in the translation of Chinese poetry. He is the pioneer of the reformist school in the field of translating Chinese poems into English, in the form of prose, comparing with Xu Yuanchong's translating Chinese poems in the poetic way. Xu Yuanchong is pursuing the principle of "three-beauty", while Weng Xianliang focuses on "reappearance of images and sound, realizing the spirit of the original". Therefore, Weng Xianliang proposes seven kinds of translation methods in the process of translating the image in Tang poetry, such as literal translation, simplification, amplification, conversion, cultural equivalence, omission and liberal translation (Sheng Xue, 2015).

Take Jia Dao's *My Lord's Garden* (《题兴化园亭》) for example:

破却千家作一池，不栽桃李种蔷薇。

蔷薇花落秋风起，荆棘满庭君始知。

A thousand homes shattered: a garden laid out. Roses everywhere, but no trees that would ever bear fruit.

Come autumn, when the roses are no more and the wind rises, there will still be these pavilions-of course-choked with thorns.

What then, my lord? (Tr. Weng Xianliang)[①]

In the original poem, the image "tao li (桃李)", which can be literally translated as "peach and plum trees", stands in contrast to another image "qiang wei (蔷薇)", which literally means roses in the Western culture, the former being trees favored by the poor peasants as they can bear fruits, while the latter being romantic favored by the rich, symbolizing the love. In translating "tao li" as "tree

---

① 翁显良. 古诗英译二十八首 [J]. 外国语，1988(6): 14.

that would bear fruit" is also an example of applying liberal translation method, keeping the sense of that in the original poem, despite the fact that Weng changes its form, so as to make the targeted readers easily understand the meaning the poet wants to express.

Take another look at Li Bai's *Thoughts in Retirement* (《田园言怀》):

贾谊三年谪，班超万里侯。

何如牵白犊，饮水对清流。

There was the great mind banished for being too wise.

There was the great soldier made marquis for exploits beyond the frontier.

But then there was the hermit who chose to he alone, unknown,

gazing on the clear mountain stream while his ox drank its fill. (Tr. Weng Xianliang) [1]

Before translating the original poem, the translator should understand Jia Yi, Ban Chao and Father of Chao: Jia Yi being unsuccessful in the officialdom, Ban Chao's achieving his ambition, and Father of Chao's living in seclusion, who is lofty and refined, unwilling to collaborate with Yao. The whole poem has a strong subjective color, that is, the heroic spirit and passionate feelings, rarely describing objective things in detail. Free and easy temperament, proud of independent personality, easy to move and easy to release the strong emotions, form the distinctive features of Li Bai's lyric style. So, understanding the whole poem's emotional and symbolic meaning can be more effective for the translators.

From the beginning of the title, the translator does not translate the

---

① 翁显良. 古诗英译二十八首 [J]. 外国语, 1988(6): 13.

"田园" in the word-for-word way, but directly translates it into "thoughts in retirement" as a whole image. because the word " 田 园 " is generally the pronoun of retiring from the outside world in Chinese poetry. As for the names of Jia Yi and Ban Chao, Weng Xianliang adopts the liberal translation by "the great mind" and "the great soldier", which explain the social identity and experiences of the two characters clearly, thus leaving readers the life traces of officialdom. Weng Xianliang gets rid of the surface structure of the original poem and explores the poet's deep feelings and aspirations through the reappearance of images, so the poem is transformed into one organic whole. He takes the natural rhythm of language and breaks the shackles of the original form and aims to convey its image and artistic conception. Weng Xianliang thinks that the most important in translating the classical poems into English is to keep the essence of poetry, which lies not in rhetoric, allusions, forms, but in images and the rhythm of strengthening its artistic effect. As long as the image of the original can be reproduced, it is not necessary to imitate its structure, syntax and word formation. Besides, "there was the great mind" "there was the great soldier" and "there was the hermit", alliteration in three places, keep the tradition of Chinese poetry appropriately without restriction. At the same time, the formation of paralleled sentences gets English readers to feel the emotional sublimation of the whole poem step by step.

Have a look at Li Bai's another poem *A Dirge* (《题戴老酒店》).

戴老黄泉下，还应酿大春。

夜台无李白，沽酒与何人？

Down there, master brewer, you'd still be practicing your art. But how you'd miss me, old friend! For where in the realm of eternal night could you find such a connoisseur? (Tr. Weng Xianliang) ①

In the original poem, the poet uses Li Bai, which is the identity of himself, as an image representing someone who really appreciates the wine made by the master brewer. Translating Li Bai as "such a connoisseur" means Li Bai knows a lot about the food, drinks and arts. Weng Xiaoliang uses liberal translation so that the connotation of the image is made clear to the English readers. However, " 大春 " is the synonym of the wine in the Tang Dynasty because at that period, in the middle of the name of wine is always with "春" . Weng Xiaoliang adopts the liberal translation, losing its cultural elements it's endowed with. " 黄泉 " means dying in China, which Weng Xiaoliang simply translates as "down there" , which leads the readers' misunderstanding. In order to impart the spirit of the original, it's a hard job for him to decide which image is increased and which one is deleted.

During the process of Chinese classical poetry's introduction to the Western readers, there are too many obstacles to overcome, which are manifested in the beauty of symmetry in form, harmony in phonology, beauty of the image and profoundness of the artistic conception. Weng Xianliang's "reappearance of images" by the prose style of "scatted in form but united in spirit" effectively reconciles the cognitive obstacles and contradictions in different cultural systems. Therefore, in the practice

---

① 翁显良 . 古诗英译二十八首 [J]. 外国语 , 1988(6): 11.

of translating Chinese poetry into English, we should try our best to reproduce images in different cultural backgrounds. At the same time, we should retain the cultural characteristics of the original language, display the deep connotation with simple words, and strive to make the foreign readers understand and appreciate.

5.4   Case Study of Stephen Owen

Stephen Owen (1946—) has been teaching Chinese literature in Harvard University. In his decades of academic research career, he has published 15 monographs and more than 40 papers focusing on the study of Tang poetry. He has won many awards, including Mellon distinguished achievement award in 2005, becoming a leader in the field of research on Tang poetry in America. In 1996, Stephen Owen's *An Anthology of Chinese Literature: Beginnings to 1911* (《中国文学选集》)was published. This 1 200-page masterpiece is composed of more than 600 poems from the pre-Qin to the Qing Dynasty. It integrates the great achievements of Chinese classical literature and he "undertakes almost all the translation tasks by himself". Among them, 206 poems were selected in Tang Dynasty, accounting for about three parts of the whole book. For readers who are not familiar with Tang poetry in the English world, his book "is very popular and easy to understand". He holds, "translation is a troublesome art; it is a gambling behavior for literary history. The strangeness of Chinese itself cannot be avoided." Let's probe into how Stephen Owen adopts its unique translation techniques

island where the gods of the West Sea (actually the East China Sea) live is a part of the Han Palace group, which is often referred to the Tang Palace. The annotation clarifies the metonymy in the original poem. Owen's translation is concise, accurate and vivid, which conveys the cultural connotation of the original poem's image and respects the source culture.

Take two lines of Li Shangyin's *Sui Palace* (《隋宫》) as an analysis:

紫泉宫殿锁烟霞，欲取芜城作帝家。

The halls of the palace at Lavender Springs

shut in mists and rose clouds,

but he wished to occupy City of Weeds

to serve as the Emperor's home. (Tr. Stephen Owen)[①]

In the original poem, the images "紫泉" and "烟霞" are translated as "Lavender Springs" and "rose clouds" by transplanting the original images with the related images in English culture, which not only preserves the beauty of the original images, but also conforms to the aesthetic habits of English readers. In the English readers' eyes, lavender is the ingredient for making perfume, emitting the fragrant odor. "Lavender Springs" awakens the readers' sensory organ and produces the resonance in the original poem. So, the clouds are presenting the rosy color against the palace. Hence, clouds and palace are expressing the "quietness and exquisiteness" of the poem correctly.

Let's explore the two lines of Yang Juyuan's *The Early Spring in the East of City* (《城东早春》):

---

① OWEN S. The great age of Chinese poetry: the high T'ang[M]. New Haven and London: Yale University Press, 1998:304.

and strategies to "avoid the absolute strangeness of traditional Chine

literature brought by the rigid translation" in translating the image

(Stephen Owen, 1996)

Look at Wang Wei's *Willow Waves* (《柳浪》):

分行接绮树，倒影入清漪。

不学御沟上，春风伤别离。

Lacy trees, touching in separate rows,

reflect in clear ripples upside down.

Do not copy those by the royal moat

that suffer from parting in the spring breeze. (Tr. Stephen Owen)[①]

Western readers may be puzzled about this: in this context, why peo

suffer from parting in the spring breeze? At that time, people had the habi

breaking the willows of Yugou to give his friends who are to be the milit

officials and expatriates. Here, in order to get the readers to accept, Ov

translates the title literally, "willow waves". He also makes a note for

title: "willow" has a homophonic sound as "remain" in Chinese. It is true

literal translation plus annotation will destroy the readers' reading pleas

to a certain extent; however, as for the image in Tang poetry which car

rich cultural connotation but has no equivalent English words, annotation

necessary means of compensation, otherwise it will cause the image's de

In Du Fu's *Ode to Autumn, Palace of Penglai* is also translated by translitera

plus the annotation. Its annotation borrows from the island's name,

---

① OWEN S. The great age of Chinese poetry: the high T'ang[M]. New Haven and Londor University Press,1998:56.

若待上林花如锦，出门俱是看花人。

If you wait for the flowers in royal parks

to be dense as a brocade,

When you go out your gate, you'll find everyone

is a person viewing the flowers. (Tr. Stephen Owen)[1]

Shanglin garden was the earliest place for royal hunting in Qin Dynasty. Emperor Wu of Han Dynasty expanded it according to the old garden built in Qin Dynasty. Till Tang Dynasty, it is more refined than that of the previous generation with jade railings. Owen directly abandons the image and takes its meaning, and renders it into "royal parks". Accordingly, it not only avoids the tedious annotation, but also imparts its original meaning.

From the above examples, Stephen Owen makes appropriate translation decisions, that is, comprehensive applying the translation methods of domestication/adaptation and foreignization/alienation, conveying the information contained in the original poems' images in the process of translating poetry. He once compared the national culture of the local to the food sold in the food shelf. If they want to own a space in the global culture, "they must occupy a marginal space marked by differences: they cannot be too short of national colors or too rich in national colors".[2] The local culture as well as the local knowledge can glow in the context of globalization. He makes great contribution to pushing Chinese traditional culture forward the global market. He becomes the spokesperson as Chinese cultural tradition in the West.

---

① OWEN S. An anthology of Chinese literature[M]. New York: W. W. Norton & Company, Inc., 1996: 463.
② 宇文所安. 他山的石头记：宇文所安自选集 [M]. 田晓菲，译. 南京：江苏人民出版社,2006:195.

Chapter 6　Conclusion

Poetry is the treasure of language and the quintessence of culture as the most concise literary form. Similarly, Chinese classical poetry is also a concentrated reflection of Chinese traditional culture and has enjoyed worldwide popularity in the past centuries with numerous translated versions both at home and abroad. Tang Dynasty has reached the heyday of Chinese classical poetry, and especially during Prime Tang period many great poets appeared and created many famous poems. Moreover, the Chinese classical poetry, of course including the poetry during Tang period, is much abundant with cultural elements due to the long and rich Chinese civilization. The image that is rooted and flourished in the soil of culture is expected to give its unique color and fragrance, so the cultural image is the soul of the Chinese classical poetry. It constitutes the core of the conception and creation and plays as the key to the comprehension and appreciation of poetry, and also poses great obstacles to its translation.

As an excellent cultural heritage of our country, Tang poetry is not smooth on the way to the West. Translating it into English, there are not only great differences between Chinese and English languages, but also the gap between them. As Waley said in his self-criticism of his translation, "in the face of the original, I have sat for several hours hundreds of times. Although I understand the meaning of the original work very clearly, I don't know how to use English that can reflect not only the meaning of the original words but also the emphasis, tone and eloquence of the original text they reproduced." (Ivan Morris, 1970)

Both Chinese and Western scholars have promoted the study of cultural image translation in theory as well as in practice. Based on their efforts and achievements, this book tries to probe into this issue from the perspective of Equivalence Theory, which has been proved to be a comparatively mature translation theory and has been commonly accepted in translation field. Although this theory originates from the translation practice of Bible, its core concepts of "closest natural equivalence" and "equivalent effect" have reasonability and popularity in regular translation. In brief, a feasible and effective strategy is worth of studying based on the Equivalence Theory.

The cultural image is generally translatable though quite difficult due to cultural absence and difference. A competent translator has to manipulate the cultural image at least from two aspects: semantic equivalence and aesthetic equivalence. The essential demand of a translation at the linguistic level is to transfer its meaning correctly, and an ideal criteria at the artistic level is to preserve aesthetic beauty in sense, sound and form of a poem.

For the sake of realizing the equivalent effect in image translation to the greatest extent, four main strategies of cultural image translation are put forward: preservation of original imagery with cultural overlap, adaptation of original imagery with cultural parallelism, amplification of the original image with cultural deficiency, and omission of the original image with cultural insignificance. In this book, images can be classified into many categories from the microscopic way, such as color images, flower images, cloud images, mountain images, etc. Each category must have special translation strategies, which awaits our exploration. Some other forms of images exist in Chinese classical works from other wide fields on image translation research. This study is beyond perfect due to the limited knowledge, there are still several limitations which calls for further study. The author will continue to do more translation practice and do poetry research which aims to have more profound insight into this field in the future.

Translation of Tang poetry is an energy-consuming but interesting job, and has fortunately gained great progress in theory and practice at home and abroad. Both traditional and new translational theories from different perspectives can provide plenty of resources and aspirations for systematic researches in this field. Therefore, a comparatively "ideal translation" deserves more exploration and constitutes the goal of all lovers and researchers of the Chinese classical poetry during the Tang period. Image translation, as well as poetry translation is calling for a combination between poetics and aesthetics. Meanwhile, the exchange of poetry between China and Western countries will be strengthened and will promote and push through Chinese culture to go to the world more smoothly.

In the background of "culture's going outside", from the individual translators' interests to the formulation of national translation strategies, there is a trend of pluralism coexistence. Most overseas sinologists, integrating their own academic background and personal interests, volunteer to translate Chinese literary works, including the poetry, and contribute a lot to the cultural exchange between China and overseas countries as pioneers. Apart from the government's support and participation, we should encourage qualified individual translators to actively participate in the background of Chinese culture's going outside, thus promoting the cultural complementary in the world.

Bibliography

[1] WALEY A. Translations from the Chinese[M].New York: Alfred A. Knopf, 1941.

[2] BAKER M. Rutledge encyclopedia of translation studies[M].Shanghai: Shanghai Foreign Language Education Press, 2004.

[3] NIDA E A. Language, culture and translating[M].Shanghai: Shanghai Foreign Language Education Press,1993.

[4] NIDA E A. Language and culture: contexts in translating[M]. Shanghai: Shanghai Foreign Language Education Press,2001.

[5] NIDA E A. Toward a science of translating[M]. Leiden: E.J.Brill, 1964.

[6] NIDA E A. From one language to another: functional equivalence in bible translating[M]. Nashville: Thomas Nelson Publishers,1986:132-151.

[7] POUND E. Personae[M].New York: New Directions Publishing Corporation, 1990.

[8] CATFORD J C. A linguistic theory of translation[M]. Oxford: Oxford University Press, 1965.

[9] NEWMARK P. Approaches to translation[M]. Shanghai: Shanghai Foreign Language Education Press, 2001.

[10] FRAZER R. The origin of the term "image"[J] .English Literary

History, 1960, 27(2): 149-161.

[11] SINGH G. Ezra Pound as critic[M].New York: St. Martin's Press, 1994.

[12] OWEN S. An anthology of Chinese literature[M].New York: W. W. Norton & Company, Inc., 1996.

[13] BASSNETT S, LEFEVERE A. Constructing cultures: essays on literary translation[M]. Shanghai: Shanghai Foreign Language Education Press, 2001.

[14] BASSNETT S. Translation studies[M]. Shanghai: Shanghai Foreign Language Education Press, 2012.

[15] ELIOT T S. Literary essays of Ezra Pound[M]. London: Faber and Faber Limited, 1954.

[16] MORRIS I. Madly singing in the mountains, an appreciation and anthology of Arthur Waley[M]. London: George Allen& Unwin Ltd, 1970.

[17] WALEY A. The poet Li Po[M]. London: East And West, Ltd, 1919.

[18] LEFEVERE A. Translation/history/culture: a sourcebook[M].Shanghai: Shanghai Foreign Language Education Press, 2004.

[19] Arthur Waley. A hundred and seventy Chinese poems[Z]. New York: Alfred A. Knopf, 1918.

[20] BYNNER W, KIANG K H. The jade mountain: a Chinese anthology[M]. New York: Alfred A. Knopf, 1929:59.

[21] HOUSE J. Translation[M]. Oxford: Oxford University Press, 2009:35.

[22] POPOVIC A. An anthology of studies on translation[M].Tel Aviv:Porter Institute for Poetics and Semiotics, 1980:45-61.

[23] OWEN S. The great age of Chinese poetry:the high Tang[M]. New Haven and London: Yale University Press, 1998:304.

中文参考文献

[1] 常耀信. 美国文学简史 [M]. 天津：南开大学出版社，1990.

[2] 陈良运. 诗学·诗观·诗美 [M]. 南昌：江西高校出版社，1991.

[3] 陈植锷. 诗歌意象论 [M]. 北京：中国社会科学出版社，1990.

[4] 戴毓庭. 等值论与诗歌翻译 [J]. 四川教育学院学报，2006(11):20−23.

[5] 辜正坤. 中西诗比较鉴赏与翻译理论 [M]. 北京：清华大学出版社，2003.

[6] 辜正坤. 译学津原 [M]. 郑州：文心出版社，2005.

[7] 顾正阳. 古诗词曲英译论稿 [M]. 上海：百家出版社，2003.

[8] 郭著章，江安，鲁文忠. 唐诗精品百首英译 [M]. 湖北：湖北教育出版社，1994.

[9] 金艾. 文化意象的传递和翻译 [J]. 西南农业大学学报（社会科学版），2005(3): 118−120.

[10] 李加强. 由阐释学和接受美学观意象翻译 [D]. 合肥：安徽大学，2005.

[11] 刘重德. 文学翻译十讲 [M]. 北京：中国对外翻译出版公司，1991.

[12] 屈光. 中国古典诗歌意象论 [J]. 中国社会科学，2002(3):162−171.

[13] 吴晟. 中国意象诗探索 [M]. 广州：中山大学出版社，2000.

[14] 辛献云. 诗歌翻译中意象的改变 [J]. 西安外国语学院学报，2001(2): 49−54.

[15] 谢天振. 译介学 [M]. 上海：上海外语教育出版社，1999.

[16] 许渊冲. 翻译的艺术 [M]. 北京：中国对外翻译出版公司，1984.

[17] 宇文所安. 中国文论：英译与评论 [M]. 上海：上海社会科学院出版社，2003.

[18] 翻译通讯编辑部.翻译研究论文集(1949–1983)[C].北京：外语教学与研究出版社，1984.

[19] 翁显良.古诗英译 [M].北京：北京出版社，1985.

[20] 张保红.汉诗英译中的意象再现 [J] 外国语，1994(2):22–26.

[21] 朱徽.中国诗歌在英语世界：英美译家汉诗翻译研究 [M].上海：上海外语教育出版社，2009.

[22] 朱徽.中英诗艺比较研究 [M].成都：四川大学出版社，2010.

[23] 侯文华.《月下独酌（其一）》"无情"释疑 [J].语文建设，2018(9)：56–59.

[24] 郑兴茂.《月下独酌》的音韵与意境之分析：兼评 Giles 的《月下独酌》英译文 [J].英语广场（下旬刊），2017(1)：18–20.

[25] 许渊冲.中诗英韵探胜 [M].北京：北京大学出版社，1992.

[26] 许渊冲.翻译的艺术 [M].北京：五洲传播出版社，2006:126–127.

[27] 许渊冲.唐诗三百首新译 [M].北京：中国对外翻译出版公司，1988.

[28] 黄薇.论宾纳英译《唐诗三百首》：兼论其"汉风诗"[D].北京：首都师范大学，2007.

[29] 顾正阳.古诗词曲英译文化溯源 [M].北京：国防工业出版社，2010.

[30] 孙雪.《九日齐山登高》马礼逊译文对唐诗英译的启示 [J].内蒙古农业大学学报（社会科学版），2016(3):140–144.

[31] 柏拉图.理想国 [M].郭斌和，张竹明，译.北京：商务印书馆，1986.

[32] 顾正阳.古诗词曲英译美学研究 [M].上海：上海大学出版社，2006.

[33] 李衍柱.柏拉图的诗论六说 [J].东方论坛，2007(1):23–32.

[34] 林语堂.论翻译 [C]// 罗新璋.翻译论集.北京：商务印书馆，1984:417–432.

[35] 刘宓庆.翻译美学导论 [M].北京：中国对外翻译出版公司，2005.

[36] 刘宓庆.翻译美学基本理论构想 [J].中国翻译，1986(4):19–24.

[37] 罗新璋 . 翻译论集 [C]. 北京：商务印书馆，1984.

[38] 罗志野 . 莎士比亚的诗论 [J]. 吉安师专学报 (哲学社会科学)，1997(2):43-48.

[39] 毛荣贵 . 翻译美学 [M]. 上海：上海交通大学出版社，2005.

[40] 田惠刚 . 中国古典诗词翻译原则与翻译批评 [J]. 外语教学，1994(1):43-51.

[41] 亚里士多德，贺拉斯 . 诗学·诗艺 [M]. 北京：人民文学出版社，1962.

[42] 张传彪 . 诗形·诗味·诗魂 [J]. 山东外语教学，2005(5):100-104.

[43] 蔡爱娟 . 基于数据库的唐诗宋词对比研究 [J]. 科技视界，2015(25):162-163.

[44] 党争胜 . 中国古典诗歌在国外的译介与影响 [J]. 外语教学，2012(3):96-100.

[45] 方华文 . 20 世纪中国翻译史 [M]. 西安：西北大学出版社，2005.

[46] 顾卫星 . 马礼逊与中西文化交流 [J]. 外国文学研究，2002(4): 116-120.

[47] 郝稷 . 英语世界中杜甫及其诗歌的接受与传播：兼论杜诗学的世界性 [J]. 中国文学研究，2011 (1): 119-123.

[48] 江岚 . 唐诗西传史论 [M]. 北京：学苑出版社，2009.

[49] 江岚，罗时进 . 唐诗英译发轫期主要文本辨析 [J]. 南京师大学报 (社会科学版)，2009(1): 119-125.

[50] 江岚，罗时进 . 早期英国汉学家对唐诗英译的贡献 [J]. 上海大学学报 (社会科学版)，2009(2):33-42.

[51] 何寅 . 许光华 . 国外汉学史 [M]. 上海：上海外语教育出版社，2002.

[52] 李特夫 . 20 世纪英语世界主要汉诗选译本中的杜甫诗歌 [J]. 杜甫研究学刊，2011(4): 79-86.

[53] 梁家敏 . 阿瑟·韦利为中国古典文学在西方打开一扇窗 [J]. 编辑学刊，2010(2): 66-68.

[54] 马祖毅 . 中国翻译通史 [M]. 武汉：湖北教育出版社，2006.

[55] 缪峥 . 阿瑟·韦利与中国古典诗歌翻译 [J]. 国际关系学院学报，2000(4): 50-56.

[56] 邬国平，邬晨云 . 李白诗歌的第一部英文译本：小畑薰良译《李白诗集》、译者与冯友兰等人关系及其他 [J]. 江海学刊，2009(4)：192-198.

[57] 王国强 . 庄延龄与翟理斯《华英字典》之关系 [J]. 辞书研究，2008(1)：125-129.

[58] 王洪，田军 . 唐诗百科大辞典 [M]. 北京：光明日报出版社，1990.

[59] 王辉 . 理雅各与《中国经典》[J]. 中国翻译，2003 (2)：37-41.

[60] 王燕，房燕 .《汉文诗解》与中国古典诗歌的早期海外传播 [J]. 文艺理论研究，2012(3)：45-52.

[61] 吴钧陶 . 唐诗英译的开山祖师 [N]. 文汇读书周报，2011-01-28(5).

[62] 许渊冲 . 谈唐诗的英译 [J]. 中国翻译，1983(3)：18-22+8.

[63] 许渊冲 . 文学与翻译 [M]. 北京：北京大学出版社，2003.

[64] 许渊冲 . 译文能否胜过原文 [J]. 教学研究，1982(2)：39-47.

[65] 许渊冲译 . 李白诗选 [M]. 长沙：湖南人民出版社，2007.

[66] 张晓 . 西方唐诗英译回顾 [J]. 成功（教育），2011(11)：267.

[67] 张晓 . 唐诗英译实践及理论研究回顾 [J]. 安徽文学（下半月），2011(9)：195-196.

[68] 赵晓辉 . 中国古典诗词促中外文化交流"中学西渐"谱华章 [N]. 人民日报，2010：10-22.

[69] 周建新 . 庞德的《神州集》与中国古典诗歌现代化 [J]. 山东外语教学，2010(4)：81-86.

[70] 朱炳荪 . 读 Giles 的唐诗英译有感 [J]. 外国语，1980(2)：45-46.

[71] 文殊 . 诗词英译选 [M]. 北京：外语教学与研究出版社，1989.

[72] 陈丹玉 . 从唐诗中的"云"意象看中国人的自然审美意识 [J]. 鸡西大学学报，2015(9)：106-110.

[73] 唐一鹤 . 英译唐诗三百首 [M]. 天津：天津人民出版社，2005.

[74] 吴钧陶 . 唐诗三百首 [M]. 长沙：湖南出版社，1996.

[75] 刘云飞. 中晚唐诗僧山水诗意象研究：以水、云、月意象为中心 [D]. 长沙：湖南师范学院，2015.

[76] 张双. 概念整合理论下唐诗中"山"意象的翻译研究浅析 [D]. 四平：吉林师范大学，2013.

[77] 于婷.《三字经》英译本比较研究：以翟里斯和赵彦春两个英译本为例 [D]. 呼和浩特：内蒙古大学，2016.

[78] 吕叔湘，许渊冲. 中诗英译比录 [M]. 香港：三联书店有限公司，1988

[79] 罗良功. 英诗概论 [M]. 武汉：武汉大学出版社，2009.

[80] 陈科龙. 阿瑟·韦利 (Arthur Waley) 唐诗英译新探：从唐诗内质及文化传播角度考察 [D]. 重庆：西南大学，2014.

[81] 翁显良. 古诗英译 [M]. 北京：北京出版社，1985.

[82] 张保红. 点染法：翁显良汉诗英译艺术研究 [J]. 中国外语，2011(4): 87-94+111.

[83] 王芳. 古汉诗英译的审美传达障碍分析 [J]. 外语与外语教学，2008(2):57-60.

[84] 翁显良. 意象与声律：谈诗歌翻译 [J]. 中国翻译，1982(6): 34-38.

[85] 翁显良. 古诗英译二十八首 [[J]. 外国语，1988(6):13-17.

[86] 翁显良. 情信与词达：谈汉诗英译的若干问题 [J]. 外国语，1980(5):20-25.

[87] 翁显良. 以不切为切：汉诗英译琐议之一 [J]. 外国语，1981(5):27-30.

[88] 翁显良. 浅中见深：汉诗英译琐议之二 [J]. 外国语，1981(6):24-27.

[89] 翁显良. 本色与变相：汉诗英译琐议之三 [J]. 外国语，1982(1):22-25.

[90] 翁显良. 意态由来画不成 [M]. 北京：中国对外翻译出版公司，1982.

[91] 盛雪. 翁显良古诗英译风格研究 [D]. 广州：广东外语外贸大学，2015.

[92] 宋彩菊. 古诗英译是否应得"意"忘"形"：以《春晓》两个英译本为例 [J]. 湖北广播电视大学学报，2008(6):110-111.

[93] 谭春萍. 翁显良汉诗英译思想评述 [J]. 海外英语，2016(3): 136-137..

[94] 范存忠. 中国诗及英文翻译 [J]. 外国语, 1981(5):9-26.

[95] 丰华瞻. 也谈形似与神似:读汉诗英译随感 [J]. 外国语, 1981(2): 20-24.

[96] 焦绘宏. 翻译理论与唐诗英译研究 [D]. 石家庄:河北师范大学, 2004.

[97] 孟立. 中国古典诗词中的意象及其翻译 [D]. 上海:上海外国语大学, 2004.

[98] 李颖. 唐诗英译中的意象问题研究:以庞德、韦利和许渊冲的译作为例 [D]. 长沙: 湖南师范大学, 2008.

[99] 程玉梅. 中诗英译:理论与实践 [D]. 北京:中国社会科学院, 2002.

[100] 李特夫. 陈剑静. 中国古典诗词英译中意象的处理 [J]. 四川师范学院学报 (哲学社会科学版), 2001(6): 77-79.

[101] 张雯. 意象、文化与翻译:从文化语言学角度对比研究唐诗英译 [D]. 大连:辽宁师范大学, 2004.

[102] 马伟. 宇文所安的唐诗译介 [D]. 上海:上海师范大学, 2007.

[103] 宇文所安. 他山的石头记:宇文所安自选集 [M]. 田晓菲, 译. 南京:江苏人民出版社, 2003.

[104] 魏家海. 宇文所安唐诗翻译的文化选择 [J]. 中国翻译, 2016(6): 76-81.

[105] 许渊冲编. 唐诗三百首新译 [M]. 北京:中国对外翻译出版公司, 1988.

[106] 袁行霈. 中国文学史 [M]. 北京:高等教育出版社, 2000.

[107] 海岸. 中西诗歌翻译百年论集 [C]. 上海:上海外语教育出版社, 2007.

[108] 赵娟. 唐诗英译研究 [M]. 成都:西南财经大学出版社, 2018.

[109] 詹晓娟. 李白诗歌英译历史 [M]. 成都:巴蜀书社, 2017.

[110] 陈缘梅. 从中国古诗英译看奈达的 "动态对应" 理论 [J]. 韶关学院学报, 2007(5): 129-132.